TOPAZ
Stories and Legends of Autumn, Hallowe'en, and Thanksgiving

BY VARIOUS

COMPILED BY
ADA M. SKINNER
AND
ELEANOR L. SKINNER

INTRODUCTION

Nature stories, legends, and poems appeal to the young reader's interest in various ways. Some of them suggest or reveal certain facts which stimulate a spirit of investigation and attract the child's attention to the beauty and mystery of the world. Others serve an excellent purpose by quickening his sense of humour.

Seedtime and harvest have always been seasons of absorbing interest and have furnished the story-teller with rich themes. The selections in "The Emerald Story Book" emphasize the hope and premise of the spring; the stories, legends, and poems in this volume, "The Topaz Story Book," express the joy and blessing which attend the harvest-time when the fields are rich in golden grain and the orchard boughs bend low with mellow fruit. "The year's work is done. She walks in gorgeous apparel, looking upon her long labour and her serene eye saith, 'It is good.'"

The editors' thanks are due to the following authors and publishers for the use of valuable material in this book:

To Dr. Carl S. Patton of the First Congregational Church, Columbus, Ohio, for permission to include his story, "The Pretending Woodchuck"; to Frances Jenkins Olcott for "The Green Corn Dance," retold from "The Journal of American Folk-Lore," published by Houghton, Mifflin Company; to Ernest Thompson Seton and the Century Company for "How the Chestnut Burrs Became"; to Dr. J. Dynelly Prince for permission to retell the legend of "Nipon" from "Kuloskap the Master"; to Thomas Nelson and Sons for "Weeds," by Carl Ewald; to William Herbert Carruth for the selection from "Each In His Own Tongue"; to Josephine K. Dodge for two poems by Mary Mapes Dodge; to A. Flanagan Company for "Golden-rod and Purple Aster," from "Nature Myths and Stories," by Flora J. Cooke; to J. B. Lippincott Company for "The Willow and the Bamboo," from "Myths and Legends of the Flowers and Trees," by Chas. M. Skinner; to Bobbs, Merrill Company for the selection by James Whitcomb Riley; to Lothrop, Lee, and Shepard Company for "The Pumpkin Giant," from "The Pot of Gold," by Mary Wilkins Freeman; to Raymond Macdonald Alden for "Lost: The Summer"; to the Youth's Companion for "A Turkey for the Stuffing," by Katherine Grace Hulbert, and "The News," by Persis Gardiner; to John S. P. Alcott for "Queen Aster," by Louisa M. Alcott; to G. P. Putnam's Sons for two poems from "Red Apples and Silver Bells," by Hamish Henry; to Francis Curtis and St. Nicholas for "The Debut of Daniel Webster," by Isabel Gordon Curtis; to Emma F. Bush and Mothers' Magazine for "The Little Pumpkin"; to Phila Butler Bowman and Mothers' Magazine for "The Queer Little Baker Man"; to the Independent for "The Crown of the Year," by Celia Thaxter; to Ginn and Company for "Winter's Herald," from Andrew's "The Story of My Four Friends"; to Frederick A. Stokes Company for "Lady White and Lady Yellow," from "Myths and Legends of Japan"; to the State Museum, Albany, New York, for permission to reprint the legend "O-na-tah, Spirit of the Corn," published in the Museum Bulletin; to Houghton, Mifflin Company for "The Sickle Moon," by Abbie Farwell Brown; "Autumn Among the Birds" and "Autumn Fashions" by Edith M. Thomas, "The Nutcrackers of Nutcracker Lodge" by Harriet Beecher Stowe, and "The Three Golden Apples" by Nathaniel Hawthorne; and to Duffield and Company for "The Story of the Opal" by Ann de Morgan.

EACH IN HIS OWN TONGUE

A haze on the far horizon,
The infinite, tender sky,
The rich, ripe tint of the cornfields,
And the wild geese sailing high;

And, all over upland and lowland
The charm of the golden-rod,——
Some of us call it Autumn,
And others call it—God.
William Herbert Carruth.

3

NIPON AND THE KING OF THE NORTHLAND

(Algonquin Legend)

The Summer Queen whom the Indians called Nipon lived in the land of sunshine where the life-giving beams of the mighty Sun shone all the year round on the blossoming meadows and green forests. The maiden's wigwam faced the sunrise. It was covered with a vine which hung thick with bell-shaped blossoms.

The fair queen's trailing green robe was woven from delicate fern leaves and embroidered with richly coloured blossoms. She wore a coronet of flowers and her long dusky braids were entwined with sprays of fragrant honeysuckle. Her moccasins were fashioned from water-lily leaves.

Nipon was very busy in her paradise of flowers. Every day she wandered through the green forests where she spoke words of 4 enouragement and praise to the great trees, or she glided over the meadows and helped the flower buds to unfold into perfect blossoms.

Sometimes the maiden's grandmother, whose name was K'me-wan, the Rain, came from afar to visit the land of Sunshine. The Summer Queen always welcomed her and listened carefully to the words of warning which K'me-wan solemnly gave before leaving.

"Nipon, my child, heed what I say. In thy wanderings never go to the Northland where dwells Poon, the Winter King. He is thy deadliest foe and is waiting to destroy thee. This grim old Winter King hates the fair beauty of the Summer Queen. He will cause thy green garments to wither and fade and thy bright hair to turn white like his own frost. All thy youth and strength he will change to age and weakness."

The Summer Maiden promised to heed her grandmother's warning, and for a long time she did not look in the direction of the Northland. But one day when she sat in front of her sun-bathed wigwam a strange 5 longing crept into her heart—a longing to look at the frozen Northland where Poon the Winter King reigned. Slowly she turned her eyes in the forbidden direction and there she saw a wonderful vision. The far-away Northland was flooded with sunshine. She could see the broad, shining lakes, the white mountain peaks touched with rosy mists, and the winding rivers gleaming with light.

"It is the most beautiful land I have ever seen," said Nipon.

She rose slowly and stood for some time looking at the enchanting beauty of the scene before her. Then she said, "My heart is filled with a strange longing. I shall go to visit the Northland, the Land of Poon, King of Winter."

"My daughter, remember K'me-wan's warning," whispered a voice and Nipon knew that her grandmother was speaking. "Go not to the Northland where death awaits thee. Abide in the land of Sunshine."

"I can not choose," said Nipon. "I must go to the Northland." 6

"Heed my warning! Heed my warning!" whispered the faint voice of K'me-wan, the Rain.

"I can not choose," repeated the Summer Queen. "I must go to the Northland."

2

In her delicate robe of leaves and her coronet of flowers Nipon left the Land of Sunshine and began her long journey northward. For many moons she traveled keeping her eyes fixed on the dazzling beauty of the frost king's land.

One day she noticed that the shining mountains, lakes, and rivers in the land of Poon moved onward before her. She stopped for a moment to consider the marvel and again a faint voice whispered, "Turn back, my child! Destruction awaits thee in the land of King Winter. Heed the warning of K'me-wan."

But the willful Summer Queen closed her ears to the pleading voice and proceeded on her journey. The beautiful vision no longer seemed to move away from her. Surely before long she would win her heart's desire, she would reach the beautiful land of Poon.

Suddenly fear seized the Summer Queen, for she felt that the sunshine 7 was gradually fading away. A chill wind from the distant mountain rent her frail garments and with sinking heart she saw the leaves of her robe were turning yellow, the blossoms were fading and dying. A cruel wind blew and tore to pieces her coronet of flowers. Then she noticed that her dusky braids were turning white as the frost.

"K'me-wan's warning!" she cried. "How I wish I had heeded K'me-wan's warning! The Frost King is cruel. He will destroy me! O K'me-wan, help me! Save me from destruction!"

Soon after Nipon left for the Northland her grandmother knew what had happened, for from her Skyland she saw that no smoke rose from the Summer Queen's wigwam. K'me-wan hastened to the land of Sunshine. There she saw that the blossoms on the queen's wigwam were beginning to wither, the ground was strewn with fallen petals, and the leaves of the vine had lost their shining green colour.

"A grey mist covers the face of the sun and a change is gradually 8 creeping over this beautiful land," cried K'me-wan. "I'll send my gentlest showers to refresh the woods and meadows."

But the Rain-mother failed to bring back the colour to the Summer Queen's island.

"The trees and flowers need warmth as well as moisture," sighed K'me-wan. "The leaves of the forest are beginning to turn orange, crimson, and brown. Every day there are fewer flowers in the meadows and along the banks of the brook. A great change is creeping over the land of Sunshine."

And as she sat in Nipon's wigwam, grieving, she heard the Summer Queen's cry of agony. She heard Nipon call out, "O K'me-wan! Save me from destruction."

"I'll send my bravest warriors to do battle with Poon," declared K'me-wan, standing and looking toward the Northland. "He shall match his strength with mine!"

Quickly she called together her strong warriors, South-wind, West-wind, and Warm-breeze.

"Go to the Northland, my warriors," she commanded. "Use all your 9 power to rescue Nipon from Poon, the Winter King. Fly to the Northland!"

K'me-wan's wind warriors fled like lightning to the land of Poon. But the crafty Winter King was not taken by surprise. The mighty North-wind, the biting East-wind, and the Frost-spirit, his strong chieftains, he held in readiness to do battle for possession of the Summer Queen. And when K'me-wan's warriors drew near the Northland, Poon gave his command.

"Fly to meet our foes, my warriors! They come from the land of Sunshine! Vanquish them!"

And as he spoke his chieftains saw that Poon's stalwart figure was growing gaunt and thin, and great drops of sweat were dropping from his brow.

At Winter King's command his giants flew to match their strength with K'me wan's warriors.

But the Snowflakes and Hailstones led by the Frost-spirit weakened and fell before Warm-breeze and his followers, the Raindrops. The 10 cold wind warriors of the North shook and roared as they matched strength with the mightier giants from the land of Sunshine. Then, as K'me-wan's warriors pressed nearer and nearer to the Northland, Poon the Winter King weakened and cried out in agony, "Set Nipon free or I shall perish. My warriors are vanquished by the chieftains of the land of Sunshine! Free the Summer Queen and end this strife!"

At this command from Poon, his giant warriors grew silent and fled back to the Northland, leaving K'me-wan's chieftains in possession of Nipon. Gently they led the weary Summer Queen back toward her own land. They travelled for many moons before the beams of the great sun were warm enough to restore her beauty.

Only once on her journey back to her own land did Nipon stop. It was when she reached a place enveloped in grey mists and dark clouds where the wild lightning leaped and flashed. The wind blew and the showers fell continually in this land of K'me-wan. Through the clouds and rain Nipon traveled until she reached the wigwam of the ancient Rain-mother. 11

"Forgive me, K'me-wan," said the Summer Queen humbly.

"My child, thou hast well nigh killed me," moaned K'me-wan faintly. "Thy disobedience has brought great suffering in my cherished island. My giant warriors conquered or Poon with his cruel ice scepter would have reigned king over all. Never again can I venture on such a struggle."

"Never again shall I disobey thee," declared Nipon, the Summer Queen.

"Hasten back to the land of Sunshine," said K'me-wan, rising. "There thou art sadly needed, for the leaves have changed their color and the blossoms are almost gone. Hasten back and give them new life, my daughter."

Then Nipon bade farewell to the Rain-mother and departed for the land of Sunshine. As she drew near her heart was filled with a wonderful joy and peace.

"Welcome, Nipon," laughed the warm sunbeams.

"Welcome, Nipon," sang the gentle breezes.

"Welcome, our life-giving Summer Queen," nodded the forest trees.

12

PRINCE AUTUMN

Carl Ewald

On the top of the hills in the West stood the Prince of Autumn and surveyed the land with his serious eyes.

His hair and beard were dashed with gray and there were wrinkles on his forehead. But he was good to look at, still and straight and strong. His splendid cloak gleamed red and green and brown and yellow and flapped in the wind. In his hand he held a horn.

He smiled sadly and stood awhile and listened to the fighting and the singing and the cries. Then he raised his head, put the horn to his mouth and blew a lusty flourish:

Summer goes his all-prospering way,
Autumn's horn is calling.
Heather dresses the brown hill-clay,
Winds whip crackling across the bay,
Leaves in the grove keep falling.

4

13

All the trees of the forest shook from root to top, themselves not knowing why. All the birds fell silent together. The stag in the glade raised his antlers in surprise and listened. The poppy's scarlet petals flew before the wind.

But high on the mountains and on the bare hills and low down in the bog, the heather burst forth and blazed purple and glorious in the sun. And the bees flew from the faded flowers of the meadow and hid themselves in the heather-fields.

But Autumn put his horn to his mouth again and blew:

Autumn lords it with banners bright
Of garish leaves held o'er him,
Quelling Summer's eternal fight,
Heralding Winter, wild and white,
While the blithe little birds flee before him.

The Prince of Summer stopped where he stood in the valley and raised his eyes to the hills in the West. And the Prince of Autumn took the horn from his mouth and bowed low before him. 14

"Welcome!" said Summer.

He took a step towards him and no more, as befits one who is the greater. But the Prince of Autumn came down over the hills and again bowed low.

They walked through the valley hand in hand. And so radiant was Summer that, wherever they passed, none was aware of Autumn's presence. The notes of his horn died away in the air; and one and all recovered from the shudder that had passed over them. The trees and birds and flowers came to themselves again and whispered and sang and fought. The river flowed, the rushes murmured, the bees continued their summer orgy in the heather.

But, wherever the princes stopped on their progress through the valley, it came about that the foliage turned yellow on the side where Autumn was. A little leaf fell from its stalk and fluttered away and dropped at his feet. The nightingale ceased singing, though it was eventide; the cuckoo was silent and flapped restlessly through the woods; the stork stretched himself in his nest and looked toward the South. But the princes took no heed. 15

"Welcome," said Summer again. "Do you remember your promise?"

"I remember," answered Autumn.

Then the Prince of Summer stopped and looked out over the kingdom where the noise was gradually subsiding.

"Do you hear them?" he asked. "Now do you take them into your gentle keeping."

"I shall bring your produce home," said Autumn. "I shall watch carefully over them that dream, I shall cover up lovingly them that are to sleep in the mould. I will warn them thrice of Winter's coming."

"It is well," said Summer.

They walked in silence for a time, while night came forth.

"The honeysuckle's petals fell when you blew your horn," said Summer. "Some of my children will die at the moment when I leave the valley. But the nightingale and the cuckoo and the stork I shall take with me."

Again the two princes walked in silence. It was quite still, only the owls hooted in the old oak. 16

"You must send my birds after me," said Summer.

"I shall not forget," replied Autumn.

Then the Prince of Summer raised his hand in farewell and bade Autumn take possession of the kingdom.

"I shall go to-night," he said. "And none will know save you. My splendour will linger in the valley for a while. And by-the-by, when I am far away and my reign is forgotten, the memory of me will revive once more with the sun and the pleasant days."

Then he strode away in the night. But from the high tree-top came the stork on his long wings; and the cuckoo fluttered out of the tall woods; and the nightingale flew from the thicket with her full-grown young.

The air was filled with the soft murmurings of wings.

Autumn's dominion had indeed begun on the night when Summer went away, with a yellow leaf here and a brown leaf there, but none had noticed it. Now it went at a quicker pace; and as time wore on, there came even more colours and greater splendour. 17

The lime trees turned bright yellow and the beech bronze, but the elder-tree even blacker than it had been. The bell-flower rang with white bells, where it used to ring with blue, and the chestnut tree blessed all the world with its five yellow fingers. The mountain ash shed its leaves that all might admire its pretty berries; the wild rose nodded with a hundred hips; the Virginia creeper broke over the hedge in blazing flames.

Then Autumn put his horn to his mouth and blew:

The loveliest things of Autumn's pack
In his motley coffers lay;
Red mountain-berries
Hips sweet as cherries,
Sloes blue and black
He hung upon every spray.

And blackbird and thrush chattered blithely in the copsewood, which gleamed with berries, and a thousand sparrows kept them company. The wind ran from one to the other and puffed and panted to add to the fun. High up in the sky, the sun looked gently down upon it all. 18

And the Prince of Autumn nodded contentedly and let his motley cloak flap in the wind.

"I am the least important of the four seasons and am scarcely lord in my own land," he said. "I serve two jealous masters and have to please them both. But my power extends so far that I can give you a few glad days."

Then he put his horn to his mouth and blew:

To the valley revellers hie!
They are clad in autumnal fancy dresses,
They are weary of green and faded tresses,
Summer has vanished, Winter is nigh——
Hey fol—de—rol—day for Autumn!

But, the night after this happened, there was tremendous disturbance up on the mountain peaks, where the eternal snows had lain both in Spring's time and Summer's. It sounded like a storm approaching. The trees grew frightened, the crows were silent, the wind held its breath. Prince Autumn bent forward and listened:

"Is that the worst you can do?" shouted a hoarse voice through the darkness. 19

Autumn raised his head and looked straight into Winter's great, cold eyes!

"Have you forgotten the bargain?" asked Winter.

"No," replied Autumn. "I have not forgotten it."

"Have a care," shouted Winter.

6

The whole night through, it rumbled and tumbled in the mountains. It turned so bitterly cold that the starling thought seriously of packing up and even the red creeper turned pale.

The distant peaks glittered with new snow.

And the Prince of Autumn laughed no more. He looked out earnestly over the land and the wrinkles in his forehead grew deeper.

"It must be so then!" he said.

Then he blew his horn.

Autumn's horn blew a lusty chime;
For the second time, for the second time!
Heed well the call, complying.
Fling seed to earth!
Fill sack's full girth!
Plump back and side!
Pad belt and hide!
Hold all wings close for flying!
20

Then suddenly a terrible bustle arose in the land, for now they all understood.

"Quick," said Autumn.

The poppy and the bell-flower and the pink stood thin and dry as sticks with their heads full of seed. The dandelion had presented each one of his seeds with a sweet little parachute.

"Come, dear Wind, and shake us!" said the poppy.

"Fly away with my seeds, Wind," said the dandelion.

And the wind hastened to do as they asked.

But the beech cunningly dropped his shaggy fruit on to the hare's fur; and the fox got one also on his red coat.

"Quick, now," said Autumn. "There's no time here to waste."

The little brown mice filled their parlors from floor to ceiling with nuts and beech-mast and acorns. The hedgehog had already eaten himself so fat that he could hardly lower his quills. The hare and fox and stag put on clean white woollen things, under their coats. 21 The starling and the thrush and the blackbird saw to their downy clothing and exercised their wings for the long journey.

The sun hid himself behind the clouds and did not appear for many days.

It began to rain. The wind quickened its pace: it dashed the rain over the meadow, whipped the river into foam and whistled through the trunks in the forest.

"Now the song is finished!" said the Prince of Autumn.

Then he put his horn to his mouth and blew.

Autumn's horn blew a lusty chime,
For the last time, for the last time!
Ways close when need is sorest:
Land-birds, fly clear!
Plunge, frogs, in mere!
Bee, lock your lair!
Take shelter, bear!
Fall, last leaf in the forest!

And then it was over.

The birds flew from the land in flocks. The starling and the lapwing, the thrush and the blackbird all migrated to the south.

7

Every morning before the sun rose the wind tore through the forest, 22 and pulled the last leaves off the trees. Every day the wind blew stronger, snapped great branches, swept the withered leaves together into heaps, scattered them again and, at last, laid them like a soft, thick carpet over the whole floor of the forest.

The hedgehog crawled so far into a hole under a heap of stones that he remained caught between two of them and could move neither forwards nor backwards. The sparrow took lodgings in a deserted swallow's nest; the frogs went to the bottom of the pond for good, settled in the mud, with the tips of their noses up in the water and prepared for whatever might come.

The Prince of Autumn stood and gazed over the land to see if it was bare and waste so that Winter's storms might come buffeting at will and the snow lie wherever it pleased.

Then he stopped before the old oak and looked at the ivy that clambered right up to the top and spread her green leaves as if Winter had no existence at all. And while he looked at it the ivy-flowers blossomed! They sat right at the top and rocked in the wind! 23

"Now I'm coming," roared Winter from the mountains. "My clouds are bursting with snow; and my storms are breaking loose. I can restrain them no longer."

The Prince of Autumn bent his head and listened. He could hear the storm come rushing down over the mountains. A snowflake fell upon his motley cloak ... and another ... and yet another....

For the last time he put his horn to his mouth and blew:

Thou greenest plant and tardiest,

Thou fairest, rarest, hardiest,

Bright through unending hours!

Round Summer, Winter, Autumn, Spring,

Thy vigorous embraces cling.

Look! Ivy mine, 'tis I who sing,

'Tis Autumn wins thy flowers!

Then he went away in the storm.

24

THE SCARF OF THE LADY

(A French Harvest Legend)

Translated by Hermine de Nagy

The Field of the Lady was the name which the peasants gave to a large tract of land belonging to a rich estate. The lord of the castle had given these fertile acres to his daughter and had told her to do as she pleased with the grain which the field produced. Each year at harvest time she invited the poor peasants of the neighbourhood to come and glean in her field, and take home with them as much grain as they needed for winter use.

Sometimes when the gleaners were busily at work one of them would cry out joyfully, "Ah, there comes the lady of the castle." They could see her coming in the distance, for she always wore a simple dress of white wool, and over her head was thrown a scarf of white silk 25 striped with many colours. She loved to come into the field while the people were at work and speak words of encouragement and cheer to them.

One sultry afternoon there were many peasants gleaning in the field. The lady of the castle had been with them for several hours. Suddenly she looked up into the threatening sky and said, "My friends, see what large clouds are gathering. I'm afraid we shall have a storm before long. Let us stop gleaning for to-day and seek shelter." The peasants hastened away and the lady started toward the castle.

As she drew near the green hedge which bordered the field she saw coming toward her a beautiful young woman and a fair child whose hand she held. The little boy's golden hair fell in waves over his white tunic.

"You came to glean," said the lady of the castle in her sweet voice, full of welcome. "Come then, we'll work together for a little while before the rain falls."

"Thank you," said the young woman. 26

The three began to pick up the ripe ears and pile them in small heaps. They had worked but a little while, however, when a gust of wind swept over the field and great raindrops began to fall. The thunder rumbled in the distance and streaks of lightning rent the sky.

"Come, my friends," said the lady of the castle. "We must seek shelter. See, there near the wood is a great oak, thick with foliage. Let us hasten to it and stand there until the storm is over."

In a short time they reached the tree and stood together under the shelter of its great branches.

With his chubby hand the child took hold of the end of his mother's veil and tried to cover his curly head with it.

"You shall have my scarf," said the lady of the castle, smiling.

She slipped it off, wrapped it tenderly around the dear child's head and shoulders, and kissed his fair young brow.

Suddenly the great clouds seemed to roll away. The lady of the castle stepped out from the shelter of the tree to look at the sky. The 27 storm had ceased and the birds were beginning to twitter in the trees. She stood still, looking at the wonderful golden light which flooded the harvest field. And in the calm silence there came floating through the air the sweetest music she had ever heard. At first it seemed far, far away. Then it came nearer and nearer until the air was filled with harmonious voices chanting tenderly in the purest angelic tones. She turned toward her companions and lo! they had disappeared.

In the distance there was a sound like the light fluttering of wings. The lady of the castle looked toward the hedge where she had first seen her mysterious companions. There she saw them again—the lovely woman and the golden-haired child. They were rising softly, softly upon fleecy clouds. Around them and mounting with them was a band of angels chanting a joyful Hosanna!

The marvelous vision rose slowly into the clear blue of the heavens. Then on the wet ears of grain in the harvest field the lady of the castle knelt in silent adoration, for she knew she had seen the Virgin and the Holy Child. While she worshipped in breathless silence 28 the heavenly choir halted and in clear, ringing tones the angels sang out:

"Blessed be thou!"

"Blessed be the good lady who is ever ready to help the poor and unfortunate! Blessed be this Field of Alms."

The Virgin stretched forth her hands to bless the lady and the harvest field. At the same time the Holy Child took from his head and shoulders the silk scarf which the lady of the castle had wrapped about him, and gave it to two rosy-winged cherubim. Away they flew—one to the right, the other to the left, each holding an end of the scarf which stretched as they flew into a marvelous rainbow arch across the blue vault of the sky. The Virgin and the Holy Child, followed by the angelic choir, rose slowly, slowly into the sky.

Softly and gently as wood breezes the heavenly music died away and the vision disappeared.

The lady of the castle rose to her feet. A marvelous thing had happened. The small heaps of grain gathered by the gleaners had 29 changed into a harvest richer than the field had ever produced before. Over all in the sky still shone the lovely rainbow arch—the arch of promise across the Field of Alms.

(Adapted.)
30

THE SICKLE MOON

(Tyrolean Harvest Legend)

Abbie Farwell Brown
When of the crescent moon aware
Hung silver in the sky,
"See, Saint Nothburga's sickle there!"
The Tyrol children cry.
It is a quaint and pretty tale
Six hundred summers old,
When in the green Tyrolean vale,
The peasant folk is told.
The town of Eben nestled here
Is little known to fame,
Save as the legends make it dear,
In Saint Nothburga's name.
For in this quiet country place,
Where a white church spire reared,
Nothburga dwelt, a maid of grace
Who loved the Lord and feared.
31
She was a serving little lass,
Bound to a farmer stern,
Who to and fro all day must pass
Her coarse black bread to earn.
She spun and knit the fleecy wool,
She bleached the linen white,
She drew the water-buckets full,
And milked the herd at night.
And more than this, when harvest-tide
Turned golden all the plain,
She took her sickle, curving wide,
And reaped the ripened grain.
All people yielded to the charm
Of this meek-serving maid,
Save the stern master of the farm,
Of whom all stood afraid.
For he was hard to humble folk,
And cruel to the poor,
A godless man, who evil spoke,

A miser of his store.
Now it was on a Saturday
Near to the Sabbath time,
Which in those ages far away
Began at sunset-chime.
32
Nothburga in the harvest gold
Was reaping busily,
Although the day was grown so old
That dimly could she see.
Close by her cruel master stood,
And fearsome was his eye;
He glowered at the maiden good,
He glowered at the sky.
For many rows lacked reaping, yet
The dark was falling fast,
And soon the round sun would be set
And working time be past.
"Cling—clang!" The sunset-chime pealed out,
And Sunday had begun;
Nothburga sighed and turned about——
The reaping was not done.
She laid her curving sickle by,
And said her evening hymn,
Wide-gazing on the starless sky,
Where all was dark and dim.
But hark! A hasty summons came
To drown her whispered words,
An angry voice called out her name,
And scared the nestling birds.
33
"What ho, Nothburga, lazy one!
Bend to your task again,
And do not think the day is done
Till you have reaped this grain."
"But master," spoke Nothburga low,
"It's the Sabbath time;
We must keep holy hours now,
After the sunset-chime."
And then in rage the master cried:
"The day belongs to me!
I'm lord of all the country side,
And hold the time in fee!"
"No Sunday-thought shall spoil the gain
That comes a hundred fold
From reaping of my golden grain,
Which shall be turned to gold."
"Nay, Master, give me gracious leave
The Lord's will I must keep;

Upon the holy Sabbath day
My sickle shall not reap!"
The master raised his heavy hand
To deal the maid a blow;
"Thou shalt!" he cried his fierce command,
And would have struck, when lo!
 34
Nothburga whirled her sickle bright
And tossed it in the sky!
A flash, a gleam of silver light,
As it went circling by,
And there, beside a little star
Which had peeped out to see,
The sickle hung itself afar,
As swiftly as could be!
The master stared up, wondering;
Forgetting all his rage,
To see so strange and quaint a thing——
The marvel of the age.
And she, the maid so brave and good,
Thenceforth had naught to fear,
But kept the Sabbath as she would,
And lived a life of cheer.
So when among the stars you see
The silver sickle flame,
Think how the wonder came to be,
And bless Nothburga's name.
 35

WINTER'S HERALD

Jane Andrews

In the days of chivalry, mail-clad knights, armed with shield and spear, rode through the land to defend the right and to punish the wrong. Whenever they were to meet each other in battle at the great tournaments, a herald was first sent to announce the fight and give fair warning to the opponents, that each might be in all things prepared to meet the other, and defend or attack wisely and upon his guard.

So, dear children, you must know that Winter, who is coming clad in his icy armour, with his spear, the keen sleet, sends before him a herald, that we may not be all unprepared for his approach.

It is an autumn night when this herald comes; all the warm September 36 noons have slipped away, and the red October sunsets are almost gone; still the afternoon light, shining through the two maples, casts a crimson and yellow glow on the white wall of my little room, and on the paths is a delicate carpet of spotted leaves over the brown groundwork.

It is past midnight when the herald is called; and although his knight is so fierce, loud, and blustering, he moves noiselessly forth and carries his warning to all the country round. Through the little birch wood he comes, and whispers a single word to the golden leaves that are hanging so slightly on the slender boughs; one little shiver goes through them, sends them fluttering all to the ground, and the next morning their brown, shriveled edges tell a sad story.

Through the birch wood he hurries and on to the bank of the brook that runs through the long valley; for the muskrat, who has his home under the shelving bank, must hear the news and make haste to arrange his hole with winter comforts before the brook is frozen. While he crosses the meadow the field mouse and the mole hear his warning and lay their heads together to see what is best to be done. Indeed, 37 the mole, who himself can scarcely see at all, is always of opinion that two heads are better than one in such cases.

Beyond the brook is Farmer Thompson's field of squashes. "I will not hurt you to-night," says the herald as he creeps among them; "only a little nip here and a bite there, that the farmer may see to-morrow morning that it is time to take you into the barn." The turnips stand only on the other side of the fence and cannot fail to know also that the herald has come.

But up in Lucy's flower garden are the heliotropes and fuchsias, tea roses and geraniums,—delicate, sensitive things, who cannot bear a cold word, it must have been really quite terrible what he said there; for before sunrise the beautiful plants hung black and withered and no care from their mistress, no smiles or kind words, could make them look up again. The ivy had borne it bravely, and only showed on his lower leaves, which lay among the grass, a frosty fringe, where the dew used to hang. 38

My two maples heard the summons and threw off their gay dresses, which withered and faded as they fell in heaps on the sidewalk. The next morning, children going to school scuffed ankle-deep among them and laughed with delight. And the maples bravely answered the herald: "Now let him come, your knight of the north wind and the storm and the sleet; we have dropped the gay leaves which he might have torn from us. Let him come; we have nothing to lose. His snows will only keep our roots the warmer, and his winds cannot blow away the tiny new buds which we cherish, thickly wrapped from the cold, to make new leaves in the spring." And the elm and the linden and horse-chestnut sent also a like brave answer back by the herald.

Over the whole village green went the whisperer, leaving behind him a white network upon the grass; and before the sun was up to tangle his beams in its meshes and pull it all to pieces, old widow Blake has seen it from her cottage window and said to herself: "Well, winter is coming; I must set up some warm socks for the boys to-day, and begin little Tommy's mittens before the week is out." 39

And Farmer Thompson stands at his great barn door, while yet the eastern sky is red, and tells Jake and Ben that the squashes and pumpkins and turnips must all be housed in cellar and barn before night; for a frost like this is warning enough to any man to begin to prepare for winter.

Mr. Winslow, the gardener, is working all day with matting and straw, tying up and packing warmly his tender shrubs and trees; and the climbing rose that is trained against the west end of the piazza must be made safe from the cold winds that will soon be creeping round there.

What will your mother do when she sees the white message that the herald has left in his frosty writing all over the lawn? Will she put away the muslin frocks and little pink or blue calicoes and ginghams, the straw hats, and Frank's white trousers and summer jackets, just as the trees threw aside their summer leaves?

Not quite like the trees; for your clothes can't be made new every spring out of little brown buds, but must be put away in the great 40 drawers and trunks of the clothes-press, to wait for you through the winter.

13

And see how your mother will bring out the woolen stockings, warm hoods and caps, mittens, cloaks and plaided dresses; and try on and make over, that all things may be ready. For it is with such things as these that she arms her little boys and girls to meet the knight who is coming with north wind and storm.

Old Margaret, who lives in the little brown house down at the corner, although she cannot read a word from a book, reads the herald's message as well as your mother can. But here are her five boys, barefooted and ragged, ever in summer clothes, and her husband lies back with a fever.

She can't send back so brave an answer as your mother does. But your mother, and Cousin George's mother, and Uncle James can help her to make a good, brave answer; for here is Frank's last winter's jacket, quite too small for him, just right for little Jim; and father's old overcoat will make warm little ones for two of the other boys. And 41 here are stout new shoes and woolen socks, and comfortable bedclothes for the sick man. Margaret sends a brave answer now, although this morning she was half ready to cry when she saw the message that Winter had sent.

Look about you, children, when the herald comes, and see what answers the people are giving him; I have told you a few. You can tell me many, if you will, before another year goes by.

42

JACK FROST

The door was shut as doors should be
Before you went to bed last night;
Yet Jack Frost has got in, you see,
And left your windows silver white.
He must have waited till you slept,
And not a single word he spoke,
But penciled o'er the panes and crept
Away before you woke.
And now you can not see the trees
Nor fields that stretch beyond the lane
But there are fairer things than these
His fingers traced on every pane.
Rocks and castles towering high;
Hills and dales and streams and fields,
And knights in armour riding by,
With nodding plumes and shining shields.
And here are little boats, and there
Big ships with sails spread to the breeze,
And yonder, palm trees waving fair
And islands set in silver seas.

43

And butterflies with gauzy wings;
And herds of cows and flocks of sheep;
And fruit and flowers and all the things
You see when you are sound asleep.
For creeping softly underneath
The door when all the lights are out,
Jack Frost takes every breath you breathe

14

And knows the things you think about.
He paints them on the window pane
In fairy lines with frozen steam;
And when you wake, you see again
The lovely things you saw in dream.
Gabriel Setoun.

44

THE PUMPKIN GIANT

Mary Wilkins Freeman

A very long time ago, before our grandmother's time, or our great-grandmother's, or our grandmothers' with a very long string of greats prefixed, there were no pumpkins; people had never eaten a pumpkin-pie, or even stewed pumpkin; and that was the time when the Pumpkin Giant flourished.

There have been a great many giants who have flourished since the world began, and, although a select few of them have been good giants, the majority of them have been so bad that their crimes even more than their size have gone to make them notorious. But the Pumpkin Giant was an uncommonly bad one, and his general appearance and his behaviour were such as to make one shudder to an extent that 45 you would hardly believe possible. The convulsive shivering caused by the mere mention of his name, and, in some cases where the people were unusually sensitive, by the mere thought of him even, more resembled the blue ague than anything else; indeed was known by the name of "the Giant's Shakes."

The Pumpkin Giant was very tall; he probably would have overtopped most of the giants you have ever heard of. I don't suppose the Giant who lived on the Bean-stalk whom Jack visited was anything to compare with him; nor that it would have been a possible thing for the Pumpkin Giant, had he received an invitation to spend an afternoon with the Bean-stalk Giant, to accept, on account of his inability to enter the Bean-stalk Giant's door, no matter how much he stooped.

The Pumpkin Giant had a very large, yellow head, which was also smooth and shiny. His eyes were big and round, and glowed like coals of fire; and you would almost have thought that his head was lit up inside with candles. Indeed there was a rumour to that effect amongst the common people, but that was all nonsense, of course; no one of 46 the more enlightened class credited it for an instant. His mouth, which stretched half around his head, was furnished with rows of pointed teeth, and he was never known to hold it any other way than wide open.

The Pumpkin Giant lived in a castle, as a matter of course; it is not fashionable for a giant to live in any other kind of a dwelling—why, nothing would be more tame and uninteresting than a giant in a two-story white house with green blinds and a picket fence, or even a brown-stone front, if he could get into either of them, which he could not.

The Giant's castle was situated on a mountain, as it ought to have been, and there was also the usual courtyard before it, and the customary moat, which was full of bones! All I have got to say about these bones is, they were not mutton bones. A great many details of this story must be left to the imagination of the reader; they are too harrowing to relate. A much tenderer regard for the feelings of the audience will be shown in this than in most giant stories; we will even go so far as to state in advance, that the story has a good 47 end, thereby enabling readers to peruse it comfortably without unpleasant suspense.

15

The Pumpkin Giant was fonder of little boys and girls than anything else in the world; but he was somewhat fonder of little boys, and more particularly of fat little boys.

The fear and horror of this Giant extended over the whole country. Even the King on his throne was so severely afflicted with the Giant's Shakes that he had been obliged to have the throne propped, for fear it should topple over in some unusually violent fit. There was good reason why the King shook; his only daughter, the Princess Ariadne Diana, was probably the fattest princess in the whole world at that date. So fat was she that she had never walked a step in the dozen years of her life, being totally unable to progress over the earth by any method except rolling. And a really beautiful sight it was, too, to see the Princess Ariadne Diana, in her cloth-of-gold rolling-suit, faced with green velvet and edged with ermine, with her glittering crown on her head, trundling along the avenues of the 48 royal gardens, which had been furnished with strips of rich carpeting for her express accommodation.

But gratifying as it would have been to the King, her sire, under other circumstances, to have had such an unusually interesting daughter, it now only served to fill his heart with the greatest anxiety on her account. The Princess was never allowed to leave the palace without a body-guard of fifty knights, the very flower of the King's troops, with lances in rest, but in spite of all this precaution, the King shook.

Meanwhile amongst the ordinary people who could not procure an escort of fifty armed knights for the plump among their children, the ravages of the Pumpkin Giant were frightful. It was apprehended at one time that there would be very few fat little girls, and no fat little boys at all, left in the kingdom. And what made matters worse, at that time the Giant commenced taking a tonic to increase his appetite.

Finally the King, in desperation, issued a proclamation that he would 49 knight any one, be he noble or common, who should cut off the head of the Pumpkin Giant. This was the King's usual method of rewarding any noble deed in his kingdom. It was a cheap method, and besides everybody liked to be a knight.

When the King issued his proclamation every man in the kingdom who was not already a knight, straightway tried to contrive ways and means to kill the Pumpkin Giant. But there was one obstacle which seemed insurmountable: they were afraid, and all of them had the Giant's Shakes so badly, that they could not possibly have held a knife steady enough to cut off the Giant's head, even if they had dared to go near enough for that purpose.

There was one man who lived not far from the terrible Giant's castle, a poor man, his only worldly wealth consisting in a large potato-field and a cottage in front of it. But he had a boy of twelve, an only son, who rivaled the Princess Ariadne Diana in point of fatness. He was unable to have a body-guard for his son; so the amount of terror which the inhabitants of that humble cottage 50 suffered day and night was heart-rending. The poor mother had been unable to leave her bed for two years, on account of the Giant's Shakes; her husband barely got a living from the potato-field; half the time he and his wife had hardly enough to eat, as it naturally took the larger part of the potatoes to satisfy the fat little boy, their son, and their situation was truly pitiable.

The fat boy's name was Aeneas, his father's name was Patroclus, and his mother's Daphne. It was all the fashion in those days to have classical names. And as that was a fashion as easily adopted by the poor as the rich, everybody had them. They were just like Jim and Tommy and May in these days. Why, the Princess's name, Ariadne Diana, was nothing more nor less than Ann Eliza with us.

One morning Patroclus and Aeneas were out in the field digging potatoes, for new potatoes were just in the market. The Early Rose potato had not been discovered in those days; but there was another potato, perhaps equally good, which attained to a similar degree of celebrity. It was called the Young Plantagenet, and reached a very 51 large size indeed, much larger than the Early Rose does in our time.

Well, Patroclus and Aeneas had just dug perhaps a bushel of Young Plantagenet potatoes. It was slow work with them, for Patroclus had the Giant's Shakes badly that morning, and of course Aeneas was not very swift. He rolled about among the potato-hills after the manner of the Princess Ariadne Diana; but he did not present as imposing an appearance as she, in his homespun farmer's frock.

All at once the earth trembled violently. Patroclus and Aeneas looked up and saw the Pumpkin Giant coming with his mouth wide open. "Get behind me, O my darling son!" cried Patroclus.

Aeneas obeyed, but it was of no use; for you could see his cheeks each side his father's waistcoat.

Patroclus was not ordinarily a brave man, but he was brave in an emergency; and as that is the only time when there is the slightest need of bravery, it was just as well. 52

The Pumpkin Giant strode along faster and faster, opening his mouth wider and wider, until they could fairly hear it crack at the corners.

Then Patroclus picked up an enormous Young Plantagenet and threw it plump into the Pumpkin Giant's mouth. The Giant choked and gasped, and choked and gasped, and finally tumbled down and died.

Patroclus and Aeneas, while the Giant was choking, had run to the house and locked themselves in; then they looked out of the window; when they saw the Giant tumble down and lie quite still, they knew he must be dead. Then Daphne was immediately cured of the Giant's Shakes, and got out of bed for the first time in two years. Patroclus sharpened the carving-knife on the kitchen stove, and they all went out into the potato-field.

They cautiously approached the prostrate Giant, for fear he might be shamming, and might suddenly spring up at them and Aeneas. But no, he did not move at all; he was quite dead. And, all taking turns, they hacked off his head with the carving-knife. Then Aeneas had it to 53 play with, which was quite appropriate, and a good instance of the sarcasm of destiny.

The King was notified of the death of the Pumpkin Giant, and was greatly rejoiced thereby. His Giant's Shakes ceased, the props were removed from the throne, and the Princess Ariadne Diana was allowed to go out without her body-guard of fifty knights, much to her delight, for she found them a great hindrance to the enjoyment of her daily outings.

It was a great cross, not to say an embarrassment, when she was gleefully rolling in pursuit of a charming red and gold butterfly, to find herself suddenly stopped short by an armed knight with his lance in rest.

But the King, though his gratitude for the noble deed knew no bounds, omitted to give the promised reward and knight Patroclus.

I hardly know how it happened—I don't think it was anything intentional. Patroclus felt rather hurt about it, and Daphne would have liked to be a lady, but Aeneas did not care in the least. He had the Giant's head to play with and that was reward enough for him. 54 There was not a boy in the neighbourhood but envied him his possession of such a unique plaything; and when they would stand looking over the wall of the potato-field with longing eyes, and he was flying over the ground with the head, his happiness knew no bounds; and Aeneas played so much with the Giant's head that finally late in the fall it got broken and scattered all over the field.

Next spring all over Patroclus's potato-field grew running vines, and in the fall Giant's heads. There they were all over the field, hundreds of them! Then there was consternation indeed! The natural conclusion to be arrived at when the people saw the yellow Giant's heads making their appearance above the ground was, that the rest of the Giants were coming.

"There was one Pumpkin Giant before," said they; "now there will be a whole army of them. If it was dreadful then what will it be in the future? If one Pumpkin Giant gave us the Shakes so badly, what will a whole army of them do?"

But when some time had elapsed and nothing more of the Giants 55 appeared above the surface of the potato-field, and as moreover the heads had not yet displayed any sign of opening their mouths, the people began to feel a little easier, and the general excitement subsided somewhat, although the King had ordered out Ariadne Diana's body-guard again.

Now Aeneas had been born with a propensity for putting everything into his mouth and tasting it; there was scarcely anything in his vicinity which could by any possibility be tasted, which he had not eaten a bit of. This propensity was so alarming in his babyhood, that Daphne purchased a book of antidotes; and if it had not been for her admirable good judgment in doing so, this story would probably never have been told; for no human baby could possibly have survived the heterogeneous diet which Aeneas had indulged in. There was scarcely one of the antidotes which had not been resorted to from time to time.

Aeneas had become acquainted with the peculiar flavour of almost everything in his immediate vicinity except the Giant's heads; and he naturally enough cast longing eyes at them. Night and day he wondered 56 what a Giant's head could taste like, till finally one day when Patroclus was away he stole out into the potato-field, cut a bit out of one of the Giant's heads and ate it. He was almost afraid to, but he reflected that his mother could give him an antidote; so he ventured. It tasted very sweet and nice; he liked it so much that he cut off another piece and ate that, then another and another, until he had eaten two-thirds of a Giant's head. Then he thought it was about time for him to go in and tell his mother and take an antidote, though he did not feel ill at all yet.

"Mother," said he, rolling slowly into the cottage, "I have eaten two-thirds of a Giant's head, and I guess you had better give me an antidote."

"O, my precious son!" cried Daphne, "how could you?" She looked in her book of antidotes, but could not find one antidote for a Giant's head.

"O Aeneas, my dear, dear son!" groaned Daphne, "there is no antidote for Giant's head! What shall we do?" 57

Then she sat down and wept, and Aeneas wept, too, as loud as he possibly could. And he apparently had excellent reason to; for it did not seem possible that a boy could eat two-thirds of a Giant's head and survive it without an antidote. Patroclus came home, and they told him, and he sat down and lamented with them. All day they sat weeping and watching Aeneas, expecting every moment to see him die. But he did not die; on the contrary he had never felt so well in his life.

Finally at sunset Aeneas looked up and laughed. "I am not going to die," said he; "I never felt so well; you had better stop crying. And I am going out to get some more of that Giant's head; I am hungry."

"Don't, don't!" cried his father and mother; but he went; for he generally took his own way, very like most only sons. He came back with a whole Giant's head in his arms.

"See here, father and mother," cried he; "we'll all have some of this; it evidently is not poison, and it is good—a great deal better than potatoes!"

18

Patroclus and Daphne hesitated, but they were hungry, too. Since the 58 crop of Giant's heads had sprung up in their field instead of potatoes, they had been hungry most of the time; so they tasted.

"It is good," said Daphne; "but I think it would be better cooked." So she put some in a kettle of water over the fire, and let it boil awhile; then she dished it up, and they all ate it. It was delicious. It tasted more like stewed pumpkin than anything else; in fact it was stewed pumpkin.

Daphne was inventive; and something of a genius; and next day she concocted another dish out of the Giant's heads. She boiled them, and sifted them, and mixed them with eggs and sugar and milk and spice; then she lined some plates with puff paste, filled them with the mixture, and set them in the oven to bake.

The result was unparalleled; nothing half so exquisite had ever been tasted. They were all in ecstasies, Aeneas in particular. They gathered all the Giant's heads and stored them in the cellar. Daphne baked pies of them every day, and nothing could surpass the felicity of the whole family. 59

One morning the King had been out hunting, and happened to ride by the cottage of Patroclus with a train of his knights. Daphne was baking pies as usual, and the kitchen door and window were both open, for the room was so warm; so the delicious odour of the pies perfumed the whole air about the cottage.

"What is it smells so utterly lovely?" exclaimed the King, sniffing in a rapture.

He sent his page in to see.

"The housewife is baking Giant's head pies," said the page, returning.

"What?" thundered the King. "Bring out one to me!"

So the page brought out a pie to him, and after all his knights had tasted to be sure it was not poison, and the King had watched them sharply for a few moments to be sure they were not killed, he tasted too.

Then he beamed. It was a new sensation, and a new sensation is a great boon to a king.

"I never tasted anything so altogether super-fine, so utterly magnificent in my life," cried the King; "stewed peacocks' tongues 60 from the Baltic are not to be compared with it! Call out the housewife immediately!"

So Daphne came out trembling, and Patroclus and Aeneas also.

"What a charming lad!" exclaimed the King, as his glance fell upon Aeneas. "Now tell me about these wonderful pies, and I will reward you as becomes a monarch!"

Then Patroclus fell on his knees and related the whole history of the Giant's head pies from the beginning.

The King actually blushed. "And I forgot to knight you, oh, noble and brave man, and to make a lady of your admirable wife!"

Then the King leaned gracefully down from his saddle, and struck Patroclus with his jeweled sword and knighted him on the spot.

The whole family went to live at the royal palace. The roses in the royal gardens were uprooted, and Giant's heads (or pumpkins, as they came to be called) were sown in their stead; all the royal parks also were turned into pumpkin-fields.

Patroclus was in constant attendance on the King, and used to stand 61 all day in his antechamber. Daphne had a position of great responsibility, for she superintended the baking of the pumpkin pies, and Aeneas finally married the Princess Ariadne Diana.

They were wedded in great state by fifty archbishops; and all the newspapers united in stating that they were the most charming and well-matched young couple that had ever been united in the kingdom.

The stone entrance of the Pumpkin Giant's Castle was securely fastened, and upon it was engraved an inscription composed by the first poet in the kingdom, for which the King made him laureate, and gave him the liberal pension of fifty pumpkin pies per year.

The following is the inscription in full:

"Here dwelt the Pumpkin Giant once.

He's dead the nation doth rejoice,

For, while he was alive, he lived

By e——g dear, fat, little boys."

The inscription is said to remain to this day; if you were to go there you would probably see it.

62

LADY WHITE AND LADY YELLOW

(A Legend of Japan)

Frederick Hadland Davis

The sixteen petal chrysanthemum is one of the crests of the Imperial family.

Long ago there grew in a meadow a white and a yellow chrysanthemum side by side. One day an old gardener chanced to come across them and he took a great fancy to Lady Yellow. He told her that if she would come along with him he would make her far more attractive; that he would give her delicate food and fine clothes to wear.

Lady Yellow was so charmed with what the old man said, that she forgot all about the white sister and consented to be lifted up, carried in the arms of the old gardener and to be placed in his garden.

When Lady Yellow and her master had departed, Lady White wept bitterly. Her own simple beauty had been despised; but what 63 was far worse, she was forced to remain in the meadow alone, without the companionship of her sister, to whom she had been devoted.

Day by day Lady Yellow grew more fair in her master's garden. No one would have recognized the common flower of the field, but though her petals were long and curled and her leaves so clean and well cared for, she sometimes thought of Lady White alone in the field, and wondered how she managed to make the long and lonely hours pass by.

One day a village chief came to the old man's garden in quest of a perfect chrysanthemum that he might take to his lord for a crest design. He informed the old man that he did not want a fine chrysanthemum with long petals. What he wanted was a simple white chrysanthemum with sixteen petals. The old man told the village chief to see Lady Yellow, but this flower did not please him, and, thanking the gardener, he took his departure.

On his way home he happened to enter a field when he saw Lady White weeping. She told him the sad story of her loneliness, and when she 64 had finished her tale of woe the village chief informed her that he had seen Lady Yellow and did not consider her half so beautiful as her own white self. At these cheery words Lady White dried her eyes and she nearly jumped off her little feet when this kind man told her that he wanted her for his lord's crest!

In another happy moment the happy Lady White was being carried in a palanquin. When she reached the Daimyo's palace all warmly praised her perfection of form. Great artists came from far and near, set about her and sketched the flower with wonderful skill. She soon saw her pretty white face on all the Daimyo's most precious belongings. She saw it on his armour and lacquer boxes, on his quilts and cushions and robes. She was painted floating down a stream and in all manner of quaint and beautiful ways. Every one acknowledged that the white chrysanthemum with her sixteen petals made the most wonderful crest in all Japan. While Lady White's happy face lived forever designed upon the Daimyo's possessions, Lady Yellow met with a sad 65 fate. She had bloomed for herself alone and had drunk in the visitor's praise as eagerly as she did the dew upon her finely curled petals. One day, however, she felt a stiffness in her limbs and a cessation of the exuberance of life. Her once proud head fell forward, and when the old man found her he pulled her up and tossed her upon a rubbish heap.

66

THE SHET-UP POSY

Ann Trumbull Slosson
Used by permission of Chas. Scribner and Sons.

Once there was a posy. 'Twa'n't a common kind o' posy, that blows out wide open, so's everybody can see its outsides and its insides too. But 'twas one of them posies like what grows down the road, back o' your pa's sugar-house, Danny, and don't come till way towards fall. They're sort o' blue, but real dark, and they look's if they was buds 'stead o' posies—only buds opens out, and these doesn't. They're all shet up close and tight, and they never, never, never opens. Never mind how much sun they get, never mind how much rain or how much drouth, whether it's cold or hot, them posies stay shet up tight, kind o' buddy, and not finished and humly. But if you pick 'em open, real careful, with a pin,—I've done it,—you find they're dreadful pretty inside. 67

You couldn't see a posy that was finished off better, soft and nice, with pretty little stripes painted on 'em, and all the little things like threads in the middle, sech as the open posies has, standing up, with little knots on their tops, oh, so pretty,—you never did! Makes you think real hard, that does; leastways, makes me. What's they that way for? If they ain't never goin' to open out, what's the use o' havin' the shet-up part so slicked up and nice, with nobody never seein' it? Folks has different names for 'em, dumb foxgloves, blind genshuns, and all that, but I allers call 'em the shet-up posies.

"Well, 'twas one o' that kind o' posy I was goin' to tell you about. 'Twas one o' the shet-uppest and the buddiest of all on 'em, all blacky-blue and straight up and down, and shet up fast and tight. Nobody'd ever dream't was pretty inside. And the funniest thing, it didn't know 'twas so itself! It thought 'twas a mistake somehow, thought it had oughter been a posy, and was begun for one, but wasn't finished, and 'twas terr'ble unhappy. It knew there was pretty posies 68 all 'round there, golden-rod and purple daisies and all; and their inside was the right side, and they was proud of it, and held it open, and showed the pretty lining, all soft and nice with the little fuzzy yeller threads standin' up, with little balls on their tip ends. And the shet-up posy felt real bad; not mean and hateful and begrudgin', you know, and wantin' to take away the nice part from the other posies, but sorry, and kind o' 'shamed.

"Oh, deary me!" she says,—I most forgot to say 'twas a girl posy—"deary me, what a humly, skimpy, awk'ard thing I be! I ain't more'n half made; there ain't no nice, pretty lining inside o' me, like them other posies; and on'y my wrong side shows, and that's jest plain and common. I can't chirk up folks like the golden-rod and daisies does. Nobody won't want to pick me and carry me home. I ain't no good to anybody, and I never shall be."

So she kep' on, thinkin' these dreadful sorry thinkin's, and most wishin' she'd never been made at all. You know 'twa'n't jest at fust she felt this way. Fust she thought she was a bud, like lots o' buds 69 all 'round her, and she lotted on openin' like they did. But when the days kep' passin' by, and all the other buds opened out, and showed how pretty they was, and she didn't open, why, then she got terr'ble discouraged; and I don't wonder a mite. She'd see the dew a-layin' soft and cool on the other posies' faces, and the sun a-shinin' warm on 'em as they held 'em up, and sometimes she'd see a butterfly come down and light on 'em real soft, and kind o' put his head down to 'em's if he was kissin' 'em, and she thought 'twould be powerful nice to hold her face up to all them pleasant things. But she couldn't.

But one day, afore she'd got very old, 'fore she'd dried up or fell off, or anything like that, she see somebody comin' along her way. 'Twas a man, and he was lookin' at all the posies real hard and partic'lar, but he wasn't pickin' any of 'em. Seems's if he was lookin' for somethin' diff'rent from what he see, and the poor little shet-up posy begun to wonder what he was arter. Bimeby she braced up, and she asked him about it in her shet-up, whisp'rin' voice. And says he, the man says: "I'm a-pickin' posies. That's what I work at 70 most o' the time. 'Tain't for myself," he says, "but the one I work for. I'm on'y his help. I run errands and do chores for him, and it's a partic'lar kind o' posy he's sent me for to-day." "What for does he want 'em?" says the shet-up posy. "Why, to set out in his gardin," the man says. "He's got the beautif'lest gardin you never see, and I pick posies for't." "Deary me," thinks she to herself, "I jest wish he'd pick me. But I ain't the kind, I know." And then she says, so soft he can't hardly hear her, "What sort o' posies is it you're arter this time?" "Well," says the man, "it's a dreadful sing'lar order I've got to-day. I got to find a posy that's handsomer inside than 'tis outside, one that folks ain't took no notice of here, 'cause 'twas kind o' humly and queer to look at, not knowin' that inside 'twas as handsome as any posy on the airth. Seen any o' that kind?" says the man.

Well, the shet-up posy was dreadful worked up. "Deary dear!" she says to herself, "now if they'd on'y finished me off inside! I'm the right kind outside, humly and queer enough, but there's nothin' worth 71 lookin' at inside,—I'm certain sure o' that." But she didn't say this nor anything else out loud, and bimeby, when the man had waited, and didn't get any answer, he begun to look at the shet-up posy more partic'lar, to see why she was so mum. And all of a suddent he says, the man did, "Looks to me's if you was somethin' that kind yourself, ain't ye?"

"Oh, no, no, no!" whispers the shet-up posy. "I wish I was, I wish I was. I'm all right outside, humly and awk'ard, queer's I can be, but I ain't pretty inside,—oh! I most know I ain't." "I ain't so sure o' that myself," says the man, "but I can tell in a jiffy." "Will you have to pick me to pieces?" says the shet-up posy. "No, ma'am," says the man; "I've got a way o' tellin', the one I work for showed me." The shet-up posy never knowed what he done to her. I don't know myself, but 'twas somethin' soft and pleasant, that didn't hurt a mite, and then the man he says, "Well, well, well!" That's all he said, but he took her up real gentle, and begun to carry her away. "Where be ye takin' me?" says the shet-up posy. "Where ye belong, 72 says the man; "to the gardin o' the one I work for," he says. "I didn't know I was nice enough inside," says the shet-up posy, very soft and still. "They most gen'ally don't," says the man.

73

THE GAY LITTLE KING

Mary Stewart

So gay it looked, that young maple tree standing in the centre of the pasture with rows and rows of dark cedars and hemlocks growing all around it! They towered above the little maple and yet seemed to bow before it, as with their size and strength they shielded it from the wind which tossed their branches. It was covered, this small tree, with leaves of flaming crimson and gold which danced and fluttered merrily in the sunshine.

"Is it after all only a maple tree?" thought the little lad Jamie, who lay upon the ground in the old pasture watching. Ever since the frost in a single night had painted the leaves with splendour, that young tree had been a real comrade to the cripple boy. Jamie had hurt his back the year before, and this summer, while the other boys 74 climbed mountains and swam streams, Jamie could only hobble upon his crutches as far as the pasture. There he lay for hours upon the grass watching the clouds drift across the sky and wishing he were a cloud or a bird, so he could fly also. The days seemed very long, and to make them pass more quickly Jamie made up stories about the mountains in the distance, the stream which rippled at the foot of the pasture and the dark evergreen trees which surrounded that flaming maple. "They are dull old courtiers, and he is a gay little king in his coronation robes," thought the boy and then—he sat up in astonishment and rubbed his eyes. Was he dreaming? No, it was all real, the young maple was gone and in its place was a little king! A crown of gleaming jewels was upon his head, he was dressed in robes of flaming crimson and over all was flung a mantle of woven gold. And the dark evergreens, where were they? There was no sign of them, and around the king stood a throng of grave and solemn courtiers dressed in green velvet, all gazing frowningly at the King. He was stamping 75 his foot, Jamie heard the stamp, and then he heard the King cry in a clear, boyish voice, "I won't be a King! I won't sit upon a throne all day long and make laws and punish people and be bowed down to; I want to be a little boy and have fun, I do!"

At that moment a gust of wind blew the King's mantle from his shoulders; it looked like a handful of golden leaves flying through the air, and the King himself—or was it only a branch of scarlet leaves?—no, it was the little King who came scampering over the grass toward Jamie. "Come," he said gleefully, "we are going to run away, you and I. We're going to have the merriest day of our whole lives!"

"But my crutches," sighed Jamie. "See, I can't run."

"Can't you?" whispered the little King gently. "Close your eyes and keep tight hold of my hand."

As Jamie shut his eyes he felt something very soft, like a bit of thistle down against his cheek, and then as light as that same thistle he felt himself rising from the ground, drifting, floating, 76 flying, up, up——"Now open your eyes," said the little King's laughing voice. Jamie obeyed, and for a moment he was puzzled. Was he a King, too, he wondered, for his clothes were of crimson velvet like the lad's beside him, or were they but leaves fluttering through the air?

"Never mind what you are," cried the King, reading his look of bewilderment. "We can all be lots more things than we dream of until the Spirit of Autumn takes hold of us. The folks below think us only leaves, but we know better, and now, where shall we go? This is my last gorgeous day, for to-night Autumn flies away from the cold breath of Winter. Let's fly to the spot you wish to see more than anything else in the world."

"Flying like this is such fun that I don't care where we go," answered Jamie, then suddenly both leaves—but let us say boys—stopped drifting and gazed in wonder at the sight before them. They were in the sunshine, but a shower was falling in the distance and opposite them, across the sky, stretched a perfect rainbow. 77

"Did you ever hear of the pot of gold at the rainbow's foot?" asked Jamie excitedly. "Let's go there now and find it!"

"All right," answered the little King, "let's go there, and if we don't find the pot of gold we may find something still more wonderful."

23

Through the air they flew toward the rainbow, whose colours were paling a little in the center, but growing more and more glorious at the end.

"Shut your eyes again and hold my hand tight," said the King. "I must fill your eyes with mist or you would be blinded by the sight you are going to see. No boy has ever seen it before except in dreams."

For a moment Jamie shivered, they seemed to be passing through a thick fog, and then—"Open your eyes," cried the King. Jamie looked——

Picture to yourself a great golden hall filled with streams of colours, each as radiant as the sunshine, and yet, seen through spectacles of mist, so soft they could not dazzle your eyes. Each great sheath of colour was moving, shifting and weaving itself in and out among the others like the figure of a dancer, so quickly 78 that it was almost impossible to catch it. And yet that was just what hundreds of gay little fairies with butterfly wings and scarfs of thistle down were trying to do. Each one carried a golden pot, and as they caught one colour after another their captives rushed away, leaving a bit of colour in the fairy's hand. Hastily dropping that bit into his golden pot with a merry, tinkling laugh, the fairy was off again after another dancing, gleaming bit of rainbow.

"So there are the pots of gold," cried Jamie. "But what do the fairies do with the rainbow's colours?"

Just then a very merry sprite came tearing past, his pot brimming over with glowing crimson. "My colour is the favourite just now," he cried. "I've got one billion trees to paint and all that's left over goes to the cardinal flowers." "Mine is just as popular," sang out another fairy, his pot overflowing with gold. "There are millions of goldenrods for me to colour as well as the trees!" "And autumn loves mine too," chanted a delicate little sprite whose pot was filled with 79 violet. "Think of all the asters without which your goldenrods would be very tiresome." "And mine," rippled another, his pot filled with blue like the sea. "Autumn always wants mine! The gentians are rare because one blossom takes more colour than a thousand of spring's forget-me-nots."

Just then a flaming orange stream rushed past, and Jamie and the little king made one grab at it.

"Thieves! Robbers!" cried the colours in a whirl of fury. In a second they were all dancing madly before the eyes of the terrified boys. Then there was a crash as of thunder and the lads found themselves lying upon the ground, wet, thick, gray mist all about them. The glorious dance at the rainbow's foot had vanished.

"I suppose we deserved that," sighed Jamie, "but I did want a pocketful of colour stuff to show the boys."

"Never mind, let's fly out of this mist and have more fun!" cried the little King. Up they floated into the sunshine and they found that 80 the winds had been busy while they were gone. Almost every tree stood dark and bare—the air was full of brilliant, whispering leaves. "Winter is surely coming soon," said the little King. "Look at the spot below us where I grew." Beneath them, in the centre of the pasture, stood the maple tree, only one crimson leaf still fluttering from its branches.

"When that leaf is gone, I'll have to say good-night for many months," said the King. "Come, before that happens we'll go to the Cavern of the winds and see how Autumn plays upon them."

This time they flew upward, and now it was so cold that Jamie drew his scarlet robes close about him. Through the first thin clouds they flew; then right into a great cloud, looking like an enormous castle, they floated. It was one huge hall, so vast that Jamie couldn't see the other end, but he could hear, far, far away beyond great arches, the rumbling of a mighty organ. Crashing and thunderous it sounded until the vast hall shook and echoed with the sound. "That is Autumn playing upon the organ of the winds," said the little King, and 81 although he shouted in Jamie's ear it sounded like a whisper above the music. "When she touches the keys the winds fill the pipes and go roaring off to carry away the leaves below," he explained. "But listen—she knows the leaves have almost all fallen and now she is singing her good-night to them."

The crashing had ceased, and through the great hall echoed a slumber song, as sweet as a thrush's note at twilight, as tender as a wood-dove's call.

Jamie closed his eyes and thought of lapping waves, and sunsets, the new moon rising and the first stars blossoming in the sky.

Did he sleep there in the Winds' Cavern with the Spirit of Autumn singing good-night to her flaming world? He never knew. When he opened his eyes he found himself standing upon the doorstep of his own home! He was drawing something soft and white about him to keep out the cold and he heard a whispered "Good-night, Comrade, until next Autumn," and a flutter as of leaves flying through the air, then the house door opened and as he stood with the light of the blazing 82 fire falling upon him he heard his mother's voice:

"Why, Jamie, you're covered with snow! And, my boy, where are your crutches?"

Into the house he ran, right into his mother's outstretched arms, although his crutches were still lying out on the pasture, buried beneath the snow! And Jamie was well! Was it a gift from the Spirit of Autumn to a little lad? Just another of her precious gifts given with her flaming leaves, her wind's music, her glorious flowers. Has she not a gift for you, too, among all these? Open your eyes and your ears and find your heart's desire!

October's touch paints all the maple leaves
With brilliant crimson, and his golden kiss
Lies on the clustered hazels; scarlet glows
The sturdy oak, and copper-hued the beech.
A russet gloss lingers in the elm;
The pensile birch is yellowing apace,
And many-tinted show the woodlands all,
With autumn's dying slendours.
—Selected.
83
THE STORY OF THE OPAL

Ann de Morgan
The opal is the stone associated with the month of October.

The sun was shining brightly one day, and a little Sunbeam slid down his long golden ladder, and crept unperceived under the leaves of a large tree. All the Sunbeams are in reality tiny Sun-fairies, who run down to earth on golden ladders, which look to mortals like rays of the Sun. When they see a cloud coming they climb their ladders in an instant and draw them up after them into the Sun. The Sun is ruled by a mighty fairy, who every morning tells his tiny servants, the beams, where they are to shine, and every evening counts them on their return, to see he has the right number. It is not known, but the Sun and Moon are enemies, and that is why they never shine at the same time. The fairy of the Moon is a woman, and all her beams are tiny women, who come down on the loveliest little ladders, 84 like threads of silver. No one knows why the Sun and Moon quarrelled. Once they were very good friends. But now they are bitter enemies, and the Sunbeams and Moonbeams may not play together.

One day a little Sunbeam crept into a tree, and sat down near a Bullfinch's nest, and watched the Bullfinch and its mate.

"Why should I not have a mate also?" he said to himself. He was the prettiest little fellow you could imagine. His hair was bright gold, and he sat still, leaning one arm on his tiny ladder, and listening to the chatter of the birds.

"But I shall try to keep awake to-night to see her," said a young Bullfinch.

"Nonsense!" said its mother. "You shall do no such thing."

"But the Nightingale says she is so very lovely," said a Wren, looking out from her little nest in a hedge close by.

"The Nightingale!" said the old Bullfinch, scornfully. "Every one knows that the Nightingale was moonstruck long ago. Who can trust a word he says?" 85

"Nevertheless, I should like to see her," said the Wren.

"I have seen her, and the Nightingale is right," said a Wood-dove in its soft, cooing tones. "I was awake last night and saw her; she is more lovely than anything that ever came here before."

"Of whom were you talking?" asked the Sunbeam; and he shot across to the Bullfinch's nest. All the birds were silent when they saw him. At last the Bullfinch said, "Only of a Moonbeam, your Highness. No one your Highness would care about," for the Bullfinch remembered the quarrel between the Sun and Moon, and did not like to say much.

"What is she like?" asked the Sunbeam. "I have never seen a Moonbeam."

"I have seen her, and she is as beautiful as an angel," said the Wood-dove. "But you should ask the Nightingale. He knows more about her than any one, for he always comes out to sing to her."

"Where is the Nightingale?" asked the Sunbeam. 86

"He is resting now," said the Wren, "and will not say a word. But later, as the Sun begins to set, he will come out and tell you."

"At the time when all decent birds are going to roost," grumbled the Bullfinch.

"I will wait till the Nightingale comes," said the Sunbeam.

So all day long he shone about the tree. As the sun moved slowly down, his ladder dropped with it lower and lower, for it was fastened to the Sun at one end; and if he had allowed the Sun to disappear before he had run back and drawn it up, the ladder would have broken against the earth, and the poor little Sunbeam could never have gone home again, but would have wandered about, becoming paler and paler every minute, till at last he died.

But some time before the sun had gone, when it was still shining in a glorious bed of red and gold, the Nightingale arose, began to sing loud and clear.

"Oh, is it you at last?" said the Sunbeam. "How I have waited for you. Tell me quickly about this Moonbeam of whom they are all talking." 87

"What shall I tell you of her?" sang the Nightingale. "She is more beautiful than the rose. She is the most beautiful thing I have ever seen. Her hair is silver, and the light of her eyes is far more lovely than yours. But why should you want to know about her? You belong to the Sun, and hate Moonbeams."

"I do not hate them," said the Sunbeam. "What are they like? Show this one to me some night, dear Nightingale."

"I cannot show her to you now," answered the Nightingale; "for she will not come out till long after the sun has set; but wait a few days, and when the Moon is full she will come a little before the Sun sets, and if you hide beneath a leaf you may look at her. But you must promise not to shine on her, or you might hurt her, or break her ladder."

26

"I will promise," said the Sunbeam, and every day he came back to the same tree at sunset, to talk to the Nightingale about the Moonbeam, till the Bullfinch was quite angry.

"To-night I shall see her at last," he said to himself, for the Moon was almost full, and would rise before the Sun had set. He hid in the oak-leaves, trembling with expectation. 88

"She is coming!" said the Nightingale, and the Sunbeam peeped out from the branches, and watched. In a minute or two a tiny silver ladder like a thread was placed among the leaves, near the Nightingale's nest, and down it came the Moonbeam, and our little Sunbeam looked out and saw her.

She did not at all look as he had expected she would, but he agreed with the Nightingale that she was the loveliest thing he had ever seen. She was all silver, and pale greeny blue. Her hair and eyes shone like stars. All the Sunbeams looked bright, and hot, but she looked as cool as the sea; yet she glittered like a diamond. The Sunbeam gazed at her in surprise, unable to say a word, till all at once he saw that his little ladder was bending. The sun was sinking, and he had only just time to scramble back, and draw his ladder after him.

The Moonbeam only saw his light vanishing, and did not see him.

"To whom were you talking, dear Nightingale?" she asked, putting her 89 beautiful white arms round his neck, and leaning her head on his bosom.

"To a Sunbeam," answered the Nightingale. "Ah, how beautiful he is! I was telling him about you. He longs to see you."

"I have never seen a Sunbeam," said the Moonbeam, wistfully. "I should like to see one so much;" and all night long she sat close beside the Nightingale, with her head leaning on his breast whilst he sang to her of the Sunbeam; and his song was so loud and clear that it awoke the Bullfinch, who flew into a rage, and declared that if it went on any longer she would speak to the Owl about it, and have it stopped. For the Owl was chief judge, and always ate the little birds when they did not behave themselves.

But the Nightingale never ceased, and the Moonbeam listened till the tears rose in her eyes and her lips quivered.

"To-night, then, I shall see him," whispered the Moonbeam, as she kissed the Nightingale, and bid him adieu. 90

"And to-night he will see you," said the Nightingale, as he settled to rest among the leaves.

All that next day was cloudy, and the Sun did not shine, but towards evening the clouds passed away and the Sun came forth, and no sooner had it appeared than the Nightingale saw our Sunbeam's ladder placed close to his nest, and in an instant the Sunbeam was beside him.

"Dear, dear Nightingale," he said, "you are right. She is more lovely than the dawn. I have thought of her all night and all day. Tell me, will she come again to-night? I will wait to see her."

"Yes, she will come, and you may speak to her, but you must not touch her," said the Nightingale; and then they were silent and waited.

Underneath the oak-tree lay a large white Stone, a common white Stone, neither beautiful nor useful, for it lay there where it had fallen, and bitterly lamented that it had no object in life. It never spoke to the birds, who scarcely knew it could speak; but sometimes, 91 if the Nightingale lighted upon it, and touched it with his soft breast, or the Moonbeam shone upon it, it felt as if it would break with grief that it should be so stupid and useless. It watched the Sunbeams and Moonbeams come down on their ladders, and wondered that none of the birds but the Nightingale thought the Moonbeam beautiful. That evening, as the Sunbeam sat waiting, the Stone watched it eagerly, and when the Moonbeam placed her tiny ladder among the leaves, and slid down it, it listened to all that was said.

At first the Moonbeam did not speak, for she did not see the Sunbeam, but she came close to the Nightingale, and kissed it as usual.

"Have you seen him again?" she asked. And, on hearing this, the Sunbeam shot out from among the green leaves, and stood before her.

For a few minutes she was silent; then she began to shiver and sob, and drew nearer to the Nightingale, and if the Sunbeam tried to approach her, she climbed up her ladder, and went farther still. 92

"Do not be frightened, dearest Moonbeam," cried he piteously; "I would not, indeed, do you any harm, you are so very lovely, and I love you so much."

The Moonbeam turned away, sobbing.

"I do not want you to leave me," she said, "for if you touch me I shall die. It would have been much better for you not to have seen me; and now I cannot go back and be happy in the Moon, for I shall be always thinking of you."

"I do not care if I die or not, now that I have seen you; and see," said the Sunbeam sadly, "my end is sure, for the Sun is fast sinking, and I shall not return to it, I shall stay with you."

"Go, while you have time," cried the Moonbeam. But even as she spoke the Sun sank beneath the horizon, and the tiny gold ladder of the Sunbeam broke with a snap, and the two sides fell to earth and melted away.

"See," said the Sunbeam, "I cannot return now, neither do I wish it. I will remain here with you till I die."

"No, no," cried the Moonbeam. "Oh, I shall have killed you! What 93 shall I do? And look, there are clouds drifting near the Moon; if one of them floats across my ladder it will break it. But I cannot go and leave you here;" and she leaned across the leaves to where the Sunbeam sat, and looked into his eyes. But the Nightingale saw that a tiny white cloud was sailing close by the Moon—a little cloud no bigger than a spot of white wool, but quite big and strong enough to break the Moonbeam's little ladder.

"Go, go at once. See! your ladder will break," he sang to her; but she did not notice him, but sat watching the Sunbeam sadly. For a moment the moon's light was obscured, as the tiny cloud sailed past it; then the little silver ladder fell to earth, broken in two and shrunk away, but the Moonbeam did not heed it.

"It does not matter," she said, "for I should never have gone back and left you here, now that I have seen you."

So all night long they sat together in the oak tree, and the Nightingale sang to them, and the other birds grumbled that he kept 94 them awake. But the two were very happy, though the Sunbeam knew he was growing paler every moment, for he could not live twenty-four hours away from the Sun.

When the dawn began to appear, the Moonbeam shivered and trembled.

"The strong Sun," she said, "would kill me, but I fear something even worse than the Sun. See how heavy the clouds are! Surely it is going to rain, and rain would kill us both at once. Oh, where can we look for shelter before it comes?"

The Sunbeam looked up, and saw that the rain was coming.

"Come," he said, "let us go;" and they wandered out into the forest, and sought for a sheltering place, but every moment they grew weaker.

When they were gone, the Stone looked up at the Nightingale, and said:

"Oh, why did they go? I like to hear them talk, and they are so pretty; they can find no shelter out there, and they will die at once. See! in my side there is a large hole where it is quite dark, and into which no rain can come. Fly after them and tell them to 95 come, that I will shelter them." So the Nightingale spread his wings, and flew, singing:

"Come back, come back! The Stone will shelter you. Come back at once before the rain falls."

They had wandered out into an open field, but when she heard the Nightingale, the Moonbeam turned her head and said:

"Surely that is the Nightingale singing. See! he is calling us."

"Follow me," sang the bird. "Back at once to shelter in the Stone." But the Moonbeam tottered and fell.

"I am grown so weak and pale," she said, "I can no longer move."

Then the Nightingale flew to earth. "Climb upon my back," he said, "and I will take you both back to the Stone." So they both sat upon his back, and he flew with them to the large Stone beneath the tree.

"Go in," he said, stopping in front of the hole; and both passed into the hole, and nestled in the darkness within the Stone.

Then the rain began. All day long it rained, and the Nightingale sat 96 in his nest half asleep. But when the Moon rose, after the sun had set, the clouds cleared away, and the air was again full of tiny silver ladders, down which the Moonbeams came, but the Nightingale looked in vain for his own particular Moonbeam. He knew she could not shine on him again, therefore he mourned, and sang a sorrowful song. Then he flew down to the Stone, and sang a song at the mouth of the hole, but there came no answer. So he looked down the hole, into the Stone, but there was no trace of the Sunbeam or the Moonbeam—only one shining spot of light, where they had rested. Then the Nightingale knew that they had faded away and died.

"They could not live away from the Sun and Moon," he said. "Still, I wish I had never told the Sunbeam of her beauty; then she would be here now."

When the Bullfinch heard of it she was quite pleased. "Now, at least," she said, "we shall hear the end of the Moonbeam. I am heartily glad, for I was sick of her."

"How much they must have loved each other!" said the Dove. "I am glad 97 at least that they died together," and she cooed sadly.

But through the Stone wherein the beams had sheltered, shot up bright, beautiful rays of light, silver and gold. They coloured it all over with every colour of the rainbow, and when the Sun or Moon warmed it with their light it became quite brilliant. So that the Stone, from being the ugliest thing in the whole forest, became the most beautiful.

Men found it and called it the Opal. But the Nightingale knew that it was the Sunbeam and Moonbeam who, in dying, had suffused the Stone with their mingled colours and light; and the Nightingale will never forget them, for every night he sings their story, and that is why his song is so sad.

In sapphire, emerald, amethyst,
Sparkles the sea by the morning kissed;
And the mist from the far-off valleys lie
Gleaming like pearl in the tender sky;
Soft shapes of cloud that melt and drift,
With tints of opal that glow and shift.
Celia Thaxter.

98
LOST: THE SUMMER

Where has the summer gone?
She was here just a minute ago,
With roses and daisies
To whisper her praises——
And every one loved her so!
Has any one seen her about?
She must have gone off in the night!
And she took the best flowers
And the happiest hours,
And asked no one's leave for her flight.
Have you noticed her steps in the grass?
The garden looks red where she went;
By the side of the hedge
There's a golden-rod edge,
And the rose vines are withered and bent.
Do you think she will ever come back?
I shall watch every day at the gate
For the robins and clover,
Saying over and over:
"I know she will come, if I wait."
Raymond Macdonald Alden.
99
BY THE WAYSIDE

On the hill the golden-rod,
And the aster in the wood,
And the yellow sunflower by the brook,
In autumn beauty stood.
William Cullen Bryant.
100
THE KING'S CANDLES

Once upon a time there lived a good king who was driven from his throne by an enemy. A few faithful knights and servants fled with his majesty to a forest where they found shelter in deep, rocky caves.

The flight from the king's palace had been so hasty that the knights and servants could bring only a few things for their king's comfort. It was in the early autumn and his majesty feared it would be necessary to live in secret during the coming winter. You may be sure the king was well pleased to find his knights had brought a few warm blankets and robes. After he had praised his followers for their thoughtfulness in providing for the winter, a young page stepped forward and said, "Your Majesty, I did not bring clothing, but I brought as many candles as I could carry."

"Candles," laughed the king, "now pray tell me, lad, why you brought 101 candles. You served me well in the palace by seeing that my throne was properly lighted, but in our forest exile we shall have little use for candles, I fear."

"Sire," replied the page, "I thought that your majesty would wish to hold council in the evenings, and that I could light your throne seat with candles as was the custom in the palace."

"I fear my throne seat, as you call it, will be nothing more than a rocky ledge for some time," said the king. "See, there is one in the inner cave which will serve. So long as the candles last, my faithful lad, your king will not be obliged to hold council in darkness."

"So long as the candles last," repeated the king's page to himself. "I hope our king's soldiers, who are seeking help, will be able to drive the usurper away before winter comes."

The king and his followers soon adapted themselves to life in exile. During the daytime they hunted game which lurked in the thickets; in the evening they gathered together in the deep cave and held council. Then it was that the king sat on his rude throne lit by two candles. 102

The king's page with sinking heart saw the candles grow fewer and fewer until there were but two left. Then at last came an evening when the lights were missing from the king's throne. In a dark corner of the cave the little page sat grieving because he could not see his king's face.

It happened one morning that the lad wandered to the edge of the woodland where the highway separated the richly coloured forest trees from a stretch of meadowland where the white mist was slowly lifting. On the roadside was an old woman carrying a large sack on her bent shoulders. When she reached the place where the king's page was standing she set her sack on the ground and looked wistfully at the meadow, then at the deep ditch which separated the field from the highway.

"Shall I help you across the ditch?" asked the king's page.

"Thank you, my lad," said the old woman. "Perhaps I'd better not go across. It would be hard for me to reach the highway again. But I 103 should like a few of those tall mullein spikes. I've none in my bag so fine as those growing in the meadow."

"I'll gather some for you" said the king's page.

He leaped across the ditch, and soon filled his hands with the tall mullein spikes.

The old woman was delighted. She tucked them into her bag and said, "They make such fine winter candles. Thank you, my lad."

"Winter candles!" exclaimed the king's page.

"Aye," nodded the old woman. "Dip them in tallow, a thin coat will do—and you have candles fit for a king. Thank you kindly."

"We are in sore need of candles where I live, but——" the page stopped.

"Use mullein spikes. They make candles fit for a king, I say," and the old woman picked up her sack.

"But we have no tallow," said the lad.

"I can spare you a lump of tallow, my boy. Come along with me to my cottage," said the old woman.

So the king's page carried the sack of mullein spikes to the old 104 woman's cottage and she gave him a large lump of tallow. On his way back he leaped across the ditch again and filled his arms with tall mullein spikes. He hurried back to the cave, melted the tallow, and dipped the weeds into the liquid fat.

When the king and his party returned that evening to the cave, two tall candles were standing on the rude throne.

"See," cried the king's page, "we have a fresh supply of candles."

"Tell us where you got them," said the surprised king.

"They are made from spikes of the mullein weed," explained the king's page. Then he told his majesty about the afternoon's adventure.

"The mullein weed shall have a new name," declared the king. "It shall be called the King's Candles."

31

A few days later the king called his followers around his throne seat and said, "A message has come to me declaring that the usurper has been driven out of my country. Tomorrow we'll hold a feast in the palace, and the table shall be lighted by 'King's Candles. 105'"

Every year since that far-off time when the reigning king holds an autumn festival, the banquet table is lighted with mullein spikes dipped in tallow, and they are called the "King's Candles."

"The mullein's yellow candles burn
Over the heads of dry, sweet fern."

106

A LEGEND OF THE GOLDEN-ROD

Frances Weld Danielson
(From "Story-Telling Time." Used by permission of Pilgrims Press.)

Once there were a great many weeds in a field. They were very ugly-looking weeds, and they didn't seem to be the least bit of use in the world. The cows would not eat them, the children would not pick them, and even the bugs did not seem to like them very well.

"I don't see what we're here for," said one of the weeds. "We are not any good."

"No good at all," growled a dozen little weeds, "only to catch dust."

"Well, if that's what we're here for," cried a very tall weed, "then I say let's catch dust! I suppose somebody's got to do it. We can't all bear blueberries or blossom into hollyhocks."

"But it isn't pleasant work at all," whined a tiny bit of a weed. 107

"No whining allowed in this field," laughed a funny little fat weed, with a hump in his stalk. "We're all going to catch dust, so let's see which one can catch the most. What do you say to a race?"

The little fat weed spoke in such a jolly voice that the weeds all cheered up at once, and before long they were as busy as bees, and as happy as Johnnie-jump-ups. They worked so well stretching their stalks and spreading out their fingers that before the summer was half over they were able to take every bit of dust that flew up from the road. In the field beyond, where the clover grew and the cows fed, there was not any to be seen.

One morning, toward the end of summer, the weeds were surprised to see a number of people standing by the fence looking at them. Pretty soon some children came and gazed at them. Then the weeds noticed that people driving by called each other's attention to them. They were much surprised at this, but they were still more surprised when one day some children climbed the fence and commenced to pick them. 108

"See," cried a little girl, "how all the dust has been changed to gold!"

The weeds looked at each other, and, sure enough, they were all covered with gold-dust.

"A fairy has done it," they whispered one to the other.

But the fairies were there on the spot, and declared they had had nothing to do with it.

"You did it yourselves," cried the queen of the fairies. "You were happy in your work, and a cheerful spirit always changes dust into gold. Didn't you know it?"

"You're not weeds any more, you're flowers," sang the fairies.

"Golden-rod, golden-rod!" shouted the children.

109

GOLDEN-ROD

Pretty, slender golden-rod,
Like a flame of light,
On the quiet, lonely way,
Glows your torch so bright.
With your glorious golden staff,
Gay in autumn hours,
Now you lead to wintry rest,
All the lovely flowers.
Cheering with a joyous face,
All that pass you by,
How you light the meadows round,
With your head so high.
Anna E. Skinner.
110

THE LITTLE WEED

"You're nothing but a weed," said the children in the fall. The little weed hung its head in sorrow. No one seemed to think that a weed was of any use.

By and by the snow came and the cold winds blew. There were many hungry little birds hunting for food.

"Twit! Twit Twee!

See! See! See!"

sang a merry little bird one cold morning.

"Here is a lovely weed full of nice brown seeds!" And he made a good meal from those seeds that morning. Then three other little birds came to share the feast.

The little weed was so happy that she held her head up straight and tall again. 111

"That is what I was meant for," she said. "I am good for something. Four hungry little birds had as many seeds as they wished for their breakfast. Next year I'll grow as many seeds as I can to feed many more hungry little birds. Good-bye, little birds," she called out to the little feathery friends. "Come again next year. I'll have another dinner for you."

"Good-bye, little weed," sang the birds. "We have had a fine meal and we thank you very much. You'll see us again next year. It is so hard to get enough to eat during the cold weather, and we are grateful to you for holding your seeds for us."

"It's nice to find that one is of some use after all, isn't it?" called out the little weed to her neighbour in the next field.

—Selected.
112

GOLDEN-ROD AND PURPLE ASTER

Flora J. Cooke

Once upon a time a strange, wise woman lived in a little hut which stood on the top of a hill. She looked so grim and severe that people were afraid to go near her. It was said that she could change people into anything she wished.

One day two little girls who lived at the foot of the hill were playing together. One was named Golden Hair and the other Blue Eyes. After a while they sat down on the grassy hillside to rest.

"I should like to do something to make everybody happy," said Blue Eyes.

"So should I," said Golden Hair. "Let us ask the woman who lives on the hilltop about it. She is very wise and can surely tell us just what to do." 113

"Oh, yes," said Blue Eyes, and away they started at once.

It was a long, long walk to the top of the hill. Many times the little girls stopped to rest under the oak trees which shaded their pathway.

They could find no flowers, but they made a basket of oak leaves and filled it with berries for the wise woman.

The birds were singing in the treetops, and the squirrels were frisking about in the branches. Golden Hair and Blue Eyes stopped to laugh and talk with them.

The little girls walked on and on up the rocky pathway. After a while the sun went down, the birds stopped their singing, and the squirrels went to bed. The evening wind was resting. How still and cool it was on the hillside!

Presently the moon and stars came out. Then the frogs and toads awoke, beetles and fireflies flew about and the night music began.

Golden Hair and Blue Eyes were growing very tired, but on and on they 114 climbed until at last they reached the hut on the hilltop where the strange, wise woman lived.

"See, she is standing at the gate," said Golden Hair. "How stern she looks."

The little girls clung close together, and when they reached the gate Golden Hair said bravely, "We know you are very wise and we came to see if you would tell us how to make everyone happy."

"Please let us stay together," said timid Blue Eyes.

As she opened the gate for the children, the wise woman was seen to smile in the moonlight. Golden Hair and Blue Eyes were never seen again at the foot of the hill. The next morning beautiful, waving golden-rod and purple asters grew all over the hillside.

Some people say that these two bright flowers, which grow side by side, could tell the secret if they would, of what became of the two little girls on that moonlight night.

(Adapted.)

115

WILD ASTERS

Child
White and purple asters, watching by the brook,
Tell me where you got your starry eyes.
Asters
Dearie, in their play the baby angels took
Blossoms from the garden of the skies.
Tossed them downward to us over heaven's wall,
And we caught and kept them,—that is all.

116

SILVER-ROD

Edith M. Thomas
Who knows not Silver-rod, the lovely and reverend Golden-rod beautified and sainted, looking moonlit and misty even in the sunshine! In this soft canescent afterbloom beginning at the apex of the flower cluster and gradually spreading downward, the eye finds an agreeable relief from the recent dazzle of yellow splendour. I almost forget that the herb is not literally in bloom, that is, no longer ministered to by sunshine and dew. Is there not, perhaps, some kind of bee that loves to work among these plumy blossoms

gathering a concentrated form of nectar, pulverulent flower of honey? I gently stir this tufted staff, and away floats a little cloud of pappus, in which I recognize the golden-and silver-rods of another year, if the feathery seeds shall find hospitable lodgment in the earth. Two other 117 plants in the wild herbarium deserve to be ranked with my subject for grace and dignity with which they wear their seedy fortunes: iron-weed, with its pretty daisy-shaped involucres; and life-everlasting, which, having provided its own cerements and spices, now rests embalmed in all the pastures; it is still pleasantly odorous, and, as often as I meet it, puts me in mind of an old-fashioned verse which speaks of the "actions of the just" and their lasting bloom and sweetness. On a chill November day I fancy that the air is a little softer in places where Silver-rod holds sway and that there spirits of peace and patience have their special haunts.

A white butterfly met a thistle-ball in the airy highway. Expressions of mutual surprise were exchanged.

"Hello! I thought you were one of us," said the butterfly.

"And I," returned the thistle-ball, "took you for a white pea-blossom."

118

PIMPERNEL, THE SHEPHERD'S CLOCK

I'll go and look at the Pimpernel
And see if she thinks the clouds look well.
For if the sun shine
And 'tis like to be fine,
I'll go to the fair.
So Pimpernel, what bode the clouds in the sky;
If fair weather, no maiden so merry as I.
Now the Pimpernel flower had folded up
Her little gold star in her coral cup.
And unto the maid
A warning she said:
"Though the sun seems down
There's a gathering frown
O'er the checkered blue of the clouded sky
So, tarry at home! for a storm is nigh!"
119

A LEGEND OF THE GENTIAN

(Hungarian)

Many years ago the poor people of Hungary suffered from a terrible sickness which had afflicted them for a long time. Thousands of them had been stricken and many had died, for nothing could be found to cure them or relieve their sufferings in any way.

At last the people appealed to their good King Ladislaw for help. Messenger after messenger was sent to beg him to bring about some relief. But the good king could do nothing, and he was obliged to send the messengers away without help and without hope.

One day the king sat thinking about the needs of his people. "What can I do for my people?" he asked himself over and over again. "I have sent them away without help and without hope. God alone knows 120 what will help them. He will give me a sign. My arrow shall bring me the message." And the good king prayed that divine guidance would direct an arrow shot into the air.

35

His Majesty shot the arrow and watched where it fell. And, behold, it pierced the root of a gentian!

The king then sent his servants to gather many roots of this plant and make from them a medicine for his suffering people. And the cure was so wonderful that from that day his people have called the gentian "The Herb of King Ladislaw."

"Thou blossom bright with autumn dew,
And coloured with the heaven's own blue,
That openest when, the quiet light,
Succeeds the keen and frosty night."

121

QUEEN ASTER

Louisa M. Alcott

For many seasons the Golden-rods had reigned over the meadow, and no one thought of choosing a king from any other family, for they were strong and handsome, and loved to rule.

But one autumn something happened which caused a great excitement among the flowers. It was proposed to have a queen, and such a thing had never been heard of before. It began among the Asters; for some of them grew outside the wall beside the road, and saw and heard what went on in the great world. These sturdy plants told the news to their relations inside; and so the Asters were unusually wise and energetic flowers, from the little white stars in the grass to the tall sprays tossing their purple plumes above the mossy wall. 122

"Things are moving in the great world, and it is time we made a change in our little one," said one of the roadside Asters, after a long talk with a wandering wind. "Matters are not going well in the meadow; for the Golden-rods rule, and they care only for money and power, as their name shows. Now, we are descended from the stars, and are both wise and good, and our tribe is even larger than the Golden-rod tribe; so it is but fair that we should take our turn at governing. It will soon be time to choose, and I propose our stately cousin, Violet Aster, for queen this year. Whoever agrees with me, say Aye."

Quite a shout went up from all the Asters; and the late Clovers and Buttercups joined in it, for they were honest, sensible flowers, and liked fair play. To their great delight the Pitcher-plant, or Forefathers' Cup, said "Aye" most decidedly, and that impressed all the other plants; for this fine family came over in the Mayflower, and was much honoured everywhere.

But the proud Cardinals by the brook blushed with shame at the idea of a queen; the Fringed Gentians shut their blue eyes that 123 they might not see the bold Asters; and Clematis fainted away in the grass, she was so shocked. The Golden-rods laughed scornfully, and were much amused at the suggestion to put them off the throne where they had ruled so long.

"Let those discontented Asters try it," they said. "No one will vote for that foolish Violet, and things will go on as they always have done; so, dear friends, don't be troubled, but help us elect our handsome cousin who was born in the palace this year."

In the middle of the meadow stood a beautiful maple, and at its foot lay a large rock overgrown by a wild grapevine. All kinds of flowers sprang up here; and this autumn a tall spray of Golden-rod and a lovely violet Aster grew almost side by side, with only a screen of ferns between them. This was called the palace; and seeing their cousin there made the Asters feel that their turn had come, and many of the other flowers agreed with them that a change of rulers ought to be made for the good of the kingdom. 124

So when the day came to choose, there was great excitement as the wind went about collecting the votes. The Golden-rods, Cardinals, Gentians, Clematis, and Bitter-sweet voted for the Prince, as they called the handsome fellow by the rock. All the Asters, Buttercups, Clovers, and Pitcher-plants voted for Violet; and to the surprise of the meadow the Maple dropped a leaf, and the Rock gave a bit of lichen for her also. They seldom took part in the affairs of the flower people,—the tree living so high above them, busy with its own music, and the rock being so old that it seemed lost in meditation most of the time; but they liked the idea of a queen (for one was a poet, the other a philosopher), and both believed in gentle Violet.

Their votes won the day, and with loud rejoicing by her friends she was proclaimed queen of the meadow and welcomed to her throne.

"We will never go to Court or notice her in any way," cried the haughty Cardinals, red with anger.

"Nor we! Dreadful, unfeminine creature! Let us turn our backs and be 125 grateful that the brook flows between us," added the Gentians, shaking their fringes as if the mere idea soiled them.

Clematis hid her face among the vine leaves, feeling that the palace was no longer a fit home for a delicate, high-born flower like herself. All the Golden-rods raged at this dreadful disappointment, and said many untrue and disrespectful things of Violet. The Prince tossed his yellow head behind the screen, and laughed as if he did not mind, saying carelessly:

"Let her try; she never can do it, and will soon be glad to give up and let me take my proper place."

So the meadow was divided: one half turned its back on the new queen; the other half loved, admired, and believed in her; and all waited to see how the experiment would succeed. The wise Asters helped her with advice; the Pitcher-plant refreshed her with the history of the brave Puritans who loved liberty and justice, and suffered to win them; the honest Clovers sweetened life with their sincere friendship, and the 126 cheerful Buttercups brightened her days with kindly words and deeds. But her best help came from the rock and the tree,—for when she needed strength she leaned her delicate head against the rough breast of the rock, and courage seemed to come to her from the wise old stone that had borne the storms of a hundred years; when her heart was heavy with care or wounded by unkindness, she looked up to the beautiful tree, always full of soft music, always pointing heavenward, and was comforted by these glimpses of a world above her.

The first thing she did was to banish the evil snakes from her kingdom; for they lured the innocent birds to death, and filled many a happy nest with grief.

The next task was to stop the red and black ants from constantly fighting; for they were always at war, to the great dismay of more peaceful insects. She bade each tribe keep in its own country, and if any dispute came up, to bring it to her, and she would decide it fairly. This was a hard task; for the ants loved to fight, and would go on struggling after their bodies were separated from their heads, 127 so fierce were they. But she made them friends at last, and every one was glad.

Another reform was to purify the news that came to the meadow. The wind was telegraph-messenger; but the birds were reporters, and some of them very bad ones. The larks brought tidings from the clouds, and were always welcome; the thrushes from the wood, and all loved to hear their pretty romances; the robins had domestic news, and the lively wrens bits of gossip and witty jokes to relate. But the magpies made such mischief with their ill-natured tattle and evil tales, and the crows criticised and condemned every

37

one who did not believe and do just as they did; so the magpies were forbidden to go gossiping about the meadow, and the gloomy black crows were ordered off the fence where they liked to sit cawing dismally for hours at a time.

Every one felt safe and comfortable when this was done, except the Cardinals, who liked to hear their splendid dresses and fine feasts talked about, and the Golden-rods, who were so used to living in 128 public that they missed the excitement, as well as the scandal of the magpies and the political and religious arguments and quarrels of the crows.

A hospital for sick and homeless creatures was opened under the big burdock leaves; and there several belated butterflies were tucked up in their silken hammocks to sleep till spring, a sad lady-bug, who had lost all her children, found comfort in her loneliness, and many crippled ants sat talking over their battles, like old soldiers, in the sunshine.

It took a long time to do all this, and it was a hard task, for the rich and powerful flowers gave no help. But the Asters worked bravely, so did the Clovers and Buttercups and the Pitcher-plant kept open house with the old-fashioned hospitality one so seldom sees nowadays. Everything seemed to prosper, and the meadow grew more beautiful day by day. Safe from their enemies, the snakes, birds came to build in all the trees and bushes, singing their gratitude so sweetly that there was always music in the air. Sunshine and shower seemed to love to freshen the thirsty flowers and keep the grass 129 green, till every plant grew strong and fair, and passers-by stopped to look, saying with a smile:—

"What a pretty little spot this is!"

The wind carried tidings of these things to other colonies, and brought back messages of praise and good-will from other rulers, glad to know the experiment worked so well.

This made a deep impression on the Golden-rods and their friends, for they could not deny that Violet had succeeded better than any one dared to hope; and the proud flowers began to see that they would have to give in, own they were wrong, and become loyal subjects of this wise and gentle queen.

"We shall have to go to Court if ambassadors keep coming with such gifts and honours to Her Majesty; for they wonder not to see us there, and will tell that we are sulking at home instead of shining as we only can," said the Cardinals, longing to display their red velvet robes at the feasts which Violet was obliged to give in the palace when kings came to visit her. 130

"Our time will soon be over, and I'm afraid we must humble ourselves or lose all the gaiety of the season. It is hard to see the good old ways changed; but if they must be, we can only gracefully submit," answered the Gentians, smoothing their delicate blue fringes, eager to be again the belles of the ball.

Clematis astonished every one by suddenly beginning to climb the maple-tree and shake her silvery tassels like a canopy over the Queen's head.

"I cannot live so near her and not begin to grow. Since I must cling to something, I choose the noblest I can find, and look up, not down, forevermore," she said; for like many weak and timid creatures, she was easily guided, and it was well for her that Violet's example had been a brave one.

Prince Golden-rod had found it impossible to turn his back entirely upon Her Majesty, for he was a gentleman with a really noble heart under his yellow cloak; so he was among the first to see, admire, and love the modest, faithful flower who grew so near him. He could not help hearing her words of comfort or reproof to those who came to her 131 for advice. He saw the daily acts of charity which no one else discovered; he knew how many trials came to her, and how bravely she bore them.

"She had done more than ever we did to make the kingdom beautiful and safe and happy, and I'll be the first to own it, to thank her and offer my allegiance," he said to himself, and waited for a chance.

One night when the September moon was shining over the meadow, and the air was balmy with the last breath of summer, the Prince ventured to serenade the Queen on his wind-harp. He knew she was awake; for he had peeped through the ferns and seen her looking at the stars with her violet eyes full of dew, as if something troubled her. So he sang his sweetest song, and Her Majesty leaned nearer to hear it; for she much longed to be friends with the gallant Prince, because both were born in the palace and grew up together very happily till coronation time came.

As he ended she sighed, wondering how long it would be before he told her what she knew was in his heart. 132

Golden-rod heard the soft sigh, and forgetting his pride, he pushed away the screen, and whispered, while his face shone and his voice showed how much he felt.

"What troubles you, sweet neighbour? Forget and forgive my unkindness, and let me help you if I can,—I dare not say as Prince Consort, though I love you dearly; but as a friend and faithful subject, for I confess that you are fitter to rule than I."

As he spoke the leaves that hid Violet's golden heart opened wide and let him see how glad she was, as she bent her stately head and answered softly.

"There is room upon the throne for two: share it with me as King, and let us rule together."

What the Prince answered only the moon knows; but when morning came all the meadow was surprised and rejoiced to see the gold and purple flowers standing side by side, while the maple showered its rosy leaves over them, and the old rock waved his crown of vine-leaves as he said: 133

"This is as it should be; love and strength going hand in hand, and justice making the earth glad."

The lands are lit
With all the autumn blaze of golden-rod,
And everywhere the purple asters nod
And bend and wave and flit.
Helen Hunt Jackson.
134

THE WEEDS

Carl Ewald

It was a beautiful, fruitful season. Rain and sunshine came by turns just as it was best for the corn. As soon as ever the farmer began to think that things were rather dry, you might depend upon it that next day it would rain. And when he thought that he had had rain enough, the clouds broke at once, just as if they were under his command.

So the farmer was in good humour, and he did not grumble as he usually does. He looked pleased and cheerful as he walked over the field with his two boys.

"It will be a splendid harvest this year," he said. "I shall have my barns full, and shall make a pretty penny. And then Jack and Will shall have some new trousers, and I'll let them come with me to market." 135

"If you don't cut me soon, farmer, I shall sprawl on the ground," said the rye, and she bowed her heavy ear quite down towards the earth.

The farmer could not hear her talking, but he could see what was in her mind, and so he went home to fetch his scythe.

"It is a good thing to be in the service of man," said the rye. "I can be quite sure that all my grain will be cared for. Most of it will go to the mill: not that that proceeding is so very enjoyable, but it will be made into beautiful new bread, and one must put up with something for the sake of honour. The rest the farmer will save, and sow next year in his field."

At the side of the field, along the hedge, and the bank above the ditch, stood the weeds. There were dense clumps of them—thistle and burdock, poppy and harebell, and dandelion; and all their heads were full of seed. It had been a fruitful year for them also, for the sun shines and the rain falls just as much on the poor weed as on the rich corn. 136

"No one comes and mows us down and carries us to a barn," said the dandelion, and he shook his head, but very cautiously, so that the seeds should not fall before their time. "But what will become of all our children?"

"It gives me a headache to think of it," said the poppy. "Here I stand with hundreds and hundreds of seeds in my head, and I haven't the faintest idea where I shall drop them."

"Let us ask the rye to advise us," answered the burdock.

And so they asked the rye what they should do.

"When one is well off, one had better not meddle with other people's business," answered the rye. "I will give you only one piece of advice: take care you don't throw your stupid seed on to the field, for then you will have to settle accounts with me."

This advice did not help the wild flowers at all, and the whole day they stood pondering what they should do. When the sun set they shut up their petals and went to sleep; but the whole night through they were dreaming about their seed, and next morning they had found a plan. 137

The poppy was the first to wake. She cautiously opened some little trap-doors at the top of her head, so that the sun could shine right in on the seeds. Then she called to the morning breeze, who was running and playing along the hedge.

"Little breeze," she said, in friendly tones, "will you do me a service?"

"Yes, indeed," said the breeze. "I shall be glad to have something to do."

"It is the merest trifle," said the poppy. "All I want of you is to give a good shake to my stalk, so that my seeds may fly out of the trap-doors."

"All right," said the breeze.

And the seeds flew out in all directions. The stalk snapped, it is true; but the poppy did not mind about that.

"Good-bye," said the breeze, and would have run on farther.

"Wait a moment," said the poppy. "Promise me first that you will not tell the others, else they might get hold of the same idea, and then there would be less room for my seeds." 138

"I am mute as the grave," answered the breeze, running off.

"Ho! ho!" said the harebell. "Haven't you time to do me a little, tiny service?"

"Well," said the breeze, "what is it?"

"I merely wanted to ask you to give me a little shake," said the harebell. "I have opened some trap-doors in my head, and I should like to have my seed sent a good way off into the world. But you mustn't tell the others, or else they might think of doing the same thing."

"Oh! of course not," said the breeze, laughing. "I shall be as dumb as a stone wall." And then she gave the flower a good shake and went on her way.

"Little breeze, little breeze," called the dandelion, "whither away so fast?"

"Is there something the matter with you too?" asked the breeze.

"Nothing at all," answered the dandelion. "Only I should like a few words with you."

"Be quick then," said the breeze, "for I am thinking seriously of lying down and having a rest." 139

"You cannot help seeing," said the dandelion, "what trouble we are in this year to get all our seeds put out in the world; for, of course, one wishes to do what one can for one's children. What is to happen to the harebell and the poppy and the poor burdock I really don't know. But the thistle and I have put our heads together, and we have hit on a plan. Only we must have you to help us."

"That makes four of them," thought the breeze, and she could not help laughing out loud.

"What are you laughing at?" asked the dandelion. "I saw you whispering just now to the harebell and poppy; but if you breathe a word to them, I won't tell you anything."

"Why, of course not," said the breeze. "I am mute as a fish. What is it you want?"

"We have set up a pretty little umbrella on the top of our seeds. It is the sweetest little plaything imaginable. If you will only blow a little on me, the seeds will fly into the air and fall down wherever you please. Will you do so?"

"Certainly," said the breeze. 140

And hush! it went over the thistle and the dandelion and carried all the seeds with it into the cornfield.

The burdock still stood and pondered. Its head was rather thick, and that was why it waited so long. But in the evening a hare leapt over the hedge.

"Hide me! Save me!" he cried. "The farmer's dog Trusty is after me."

"You can creep behind the hedge," said the burdock, "then I will hide you."

"You don't look able to do that," said the hare, "but in time of need one must help oneself as one can." And so he got in safely behind the hedge.

"Now you may repay me by taking some of my seeds with you over into the cornfield," said the burdock; and it broke off some of its many heads and fixed them on the hare.

A little later Trusty came trotting up to the hedge.

"Here's the dog," whispered the burdock, and with one spring the hare leapt over the hedge and into the rye. 141

"Haven't you seen the hare, burdock?" asked Trusty. "I see I have grown too old to go hunting. I am quite blind in one eye, and I have completely lost my scent."

"Yes, I have seen him," answered the burdock; "and if you will do me a service, I will show you where he is."

Trusty agreed, and the burdock fastened some heads on his back, and said to him:

"If you will only rub yourself against the stile there in the cornfield, my seeds will fall off. But you must not look for the hare there, for a little while ago I saw him run into the wood." Trusty dropped the burrs on the field and trotted to the wood.

"Well, I've sent my seeds out in the world all right," said the burdock, laughing as if much pleased with itself; "but it is impossible to say what will become of the thistle and the dandelion and the harebell and the poppy."

Spring had come round once more, and the rye stood high already.

"We are pretty well off on the whole," said the rye plants. "Here we stand in a great company, and not one of us but belongs to our own 142 noble family. And we don't get in each other's way in the very least. It is a grand thing to be in the service of man."

But one fine day a crowd of little poppies, and thistles and dandelions, and burdocks and harebells poked up their heads above ground, all amongst the flourishing rye.

"What does this mean?" asked the rye. "Where in the world are you sprung from?"

And the poppy looked at the harebell and asked: "Where did you come from?"

And the thistle looked at the burdock and asked: "Where in the world have you come from?"

They were all equally astonished, and it was an hour before they had explained. But the rye was the angriest, and when she had heard all about Trusty and the hare and the breeze she grew quite wild.

"Don't be in such a passion, you green rye," said the breeze, who had been lying behind the hedge and hearing everything. "I ask no one's permission, but do as I like; and now I'm going to make you bow to me."

Then she passed over the young rye, and the thin blades swayed backwards and forwards. 143

"You see," she said, "the farmer attends to his rye, because that is his business. But the rain and the sun and I—we attend to all of you without respect of persons. To our eyes the poor weed is just as pretty as the rich corn."

(Abridged.)

144

AUTUMN FIRES

In the other gardens
And all up the vale
From the autumn bonfires
See the smoke trail!
Pleasant summer over
And all the summer flowers;
The red fire blazes,
The gray smoke towers.
Sing a song of seasons!
Something bright in all!
Flowers in the summer!
Fires in the fall!
Robert Louis Stevenson.

145

146

AMONG THE TREES

TO AN AUTUMN LEAF

Wee shallop of shimmering gold!
Slip down from your ways in the branches
Some fairy will loosen your hold——
Wee shallop of shimmering gold.
Spill dew on your bows and unfold
Silk sails for the fairest of launches!

Wee shallop of shimmering gold;
Slip down from your ways in the branches.
147

WHY THE AUTUMN LEAVES ARE RED

Emelyn Newcomb Partridge

Long, long ago no one but animals lived upon the earth and sometimes they would hold great Councils. The Bear would be there,—the Bear, with his sharp claws, and his shiny coat, and his big, big growl; and the Deer, who was so proud of his antlers, for they came out of his head like trees; and all the animals, and all the birds would be present at the great Council. Little Turtle would go there, too. She was so small that she did not like to speak to anyone. But, she often wished:

"Oh, if only I could do some good deed! What could such a little creature as I do? Anyway," she thought, "I'll be on the watch,—and it may be that some time there will be a chance for me to do something for my people." 148

Little Turtle never forgot about that good deed she had planned to perform. One day the opportunity came to her. She was at the Council, and the animals were saying:

"It is so dark here, we have only the Snowlight to see by. It is gloomy, too. Couldn't we make a light and place it up in Skyland?" they asked.

Little Turtle said: "Please let me go up to Skyland? I am sure that I can make a light shine up there."

They said that she might go, and they called Dark Cloud to carry Little Turtle there. Dark Cloud came.

Little Turtle saw that Thunder and Lightning were in Dark Cloud; and when she reached Skyland, she made the Sun from Lightning, and placed him in the Sky.

The Sun could not move, because he had no life, and all the world underneath was too hot to live upon.

"What shall we do?" the animals asked one another. Someone said:

"We must give the Sun life and spirit, and then he will move about in the sky." 149

So they gave him life and spirit, and he moved about in the sky. Mud Turtle dug a hole through the earth for the Sun to travel through. Little Turtle made a wife for him out of some of the Lightning from Dark Cloud. She was the Moon. Their little children were the stars that played all over Skyland.

All this time, Little Turtle was taking care of Skyland. The animals below called her, She Who Takes Care of Skyland. And she was very happy, because she was doing her good deed.

Some of the animals became jealous of Little Turtle,—especially the Deer, who was so proud of his antlers. One day, Deer said to Rainbow:

"Rainbow, please take me up to Skyland where Little Turtle lives."

Rainbow did not know whether it would be quite right to take Deer up to Little Turtle's house, but he said:

"In the winter, when I rest upon the big mountain by the lake, then I will take you."

This made the Deer glad. He did not tell anyone about the promise of 150 Rainbow. All winter long, he waited and watched near the big mountain for Rainbow to come; but Rainbow did not come to him. In the spring, one day, Deer saw Rainbow beside the lake.

"Rainbow," he asked, "why did you not keep your promise to me?" Rainbow made him another promise.

"Come to me by the lake, when you see me in the thick fog," he said.

The Deer kept this promise a secret, too; because he hoped to go to Skyland alone. Day after day, he waited beside the lake. One day, when the thick fog was rising from the lake,—Deer saw the beautiful Rainbow.

Rainbow made an arch from the lake to the big mountain. Then a shining light fell about the Deer, and he saw a straight path shining with all the colours of the Rainbow. It led through a great forest.

"Follow the beautiful path through the great forest," Rainbow said.

The Deer entered the shining pathway, and it led him straight to the house of Little Turtle in Skyland. And the Deer went about Skyland everywhere. 151

When the great Council met, Deer was not there. "The Deer is not come to the Council, where is the Deer?" they asked.

Hawk flew about the air everywhere, and could not find Deer in the air. Wolf searched the deep woods, and could not find Deer in the forests.

When Dark Cloud brought Little Turtle to the Council, Little Turtle told them how Rainbow had made a path for Deer to climb to Skyland. "There it is now," said Little Turtle.

The animals looked over the lake, and they saw, there, the beautiful pathway. They had never seen it before.

"Why did not Deer wait for us? All of us should have gone to Skyland together," they said.

Now, Brown Bear determined to follow that pathway the very next time he should see it.

One day when he was all alone, near the lake, he saw the shining path that led through the great forest. Soon he found himself in Skyland. The first person he met was the Deer. 152

"Why did you leave us? Why did you go to the land of Little Turtle without us? Why did you not wait for us?" he asked the Deer.

The Deer shook his antlers angrily. "What right have you to question me? No one but the Wolf may question why I came. I will kill you for your impertinence."

The Deer arched his neck; he poised his antlered head; his eyes blazed with fury.

The Bear was not afraid. He stood up; his claws were sharp and strong; his hoarse growls sounded all over Skyland.

The battle of the Deer and the Bear shook Skyland. The animals looked up from the earth.

"Who will go? Who will go to Skyland and forbid the Deer to fight?"

"I will go," said the Wolf. "I can run faster than anyone." So Wolf ran along the shining pathway, and in a little while he had reached the place of the battle. Wolf made Deer stop fighting. Deer's antlers were covered with blood, and when he shook them, great drops fell down, down through the air, and splashed against all the leaves of the forest. And the leaves became a beautiful red. 153

So, in the autumn, when you see the leaves turning red, you may know that it is because in the long ago, the Deer and the Bear fought a great battle in Skyland, in the land of Little Turtle who was doing her good deed.

154

THE ANXIOUS LEAF

Henry Ward Beecher

Once upon a time a little leaf was heard to sigh and cry, as leaves often do when a gentle wind is about. And the twig said, "What is the matter, little leaf?" And the leaf said,

"The wind just told me that one day it would pull me off and throw me down to lie on the ground!" The twig told it to the branch on which it grew, and the branch told it to the tree. And when the tree heard it, it rustled all over, and sent back word to the leaf, "Do not be afraid; hold on tightly, and you shall not go till you want to." And so the leaf stopped sighing, but went on nestling and singing. Every time the tree shook itself and stirred up all its leaves, the branches shook themselves, and the little twig shook itself, and the little leaf danced up and down 155 merrily, as if nothing could ever pull it off. And so it grew all summer long until October. And when the bright days of autumn came, the little leaf saw all the leaves around becoming very beautiful. Some were yellow, and some scarlet, and some striped with both colours. Then it asked the tree what it meant. And the tree said, "All these leaves are getting ready to fly away, and they have put on these beautiful colours because of joy." Then the little leaf began to want to go, and grew very beautiful in thinking of it, and when it was very gay in colour, it saw that the branches of the tree had no colour in them, and so the leaf said, "O branches, why are you lead colour and we golden?" "We must keep on our workclothes, for our life is not done; but your clothes are for holiday, because your tasks are over." Just then a little puff of wind came, and the leaf let go without thinking of it, and the wind took it up, and turned it over and over, and whirled it like a spark of fire in the air, and then it fell gently down under the fence among hundreds of other leaves, and began to dream—a dream so beautiful that perhaps it will last forever.

156
HOW THE CHESTNUT BURRS BECAME

Ernest Thompson Seton
In the woods of Poconic there once roamed a very discontented Porcupine. He was forever fretting. He complained that everything was wrong, till it was perfectly scandalous and the Great Spirit, getting tired of his grumbling, said:

"You and the world I have made don't seem to fit. One or the other must be wrong. It is easier to change you. You don't like the trees, you are unhappy on the ground, and think everything is upside down, so I'll turn you inside out and put you in the water."

This was the origin of the Shad.

After Manitou had turned the old Porcupine into a Shad the young ones missed their mother and crawled up into a high tree to look for her 157 coming. Manitou happened to pass that way and they all chattered their teeth at him, thinking themselves safe. They were not wicked, only ill-trained, some of them, indeed, were at heart quite good, but, oh, so ill-trained, and they chattered and groaned as Manitou came nearer. Remembering then that he had taken their mother from them, he said, "You look very well up there, you little Porkys, so you had better stay there for always, and be part of the tree."

This was the origin of the chestnut burrs. They hang like a lot of little porcupines on the tree-crotches. They are spiny, and dangerous, utterly without manners and yet most of them have a good little heart inside.

158
THE MERRY WIND

The merry wind came racing
Adown the hills one day,
In gleeful frolic chasing
The rustling leaves away.

In clouds of red and yellow,
He whirled the leaves along,
And then the jolly fellow
He sang a cheery song.
The merry wind was weary
At last of fun and play;
His voice grew faint and eerie,
And softly died away.
Far off a crow was calling
And in the mellow sun
The painted leaves kept falling
And fading, one by one.
Mary Mapes Dodge.
 159
AUTUMN AMONG THE BIRDS

[Enter a little Snipe, crying:
Peet-weet! Peet-weet!
I've such cold feet,
And nothing to eat!
The creek is so high
That I can't keep dry
Except when I fly!
Peet-weet!
[A Kildeer:
Kildee! Kildee! Kildee!
This is no place for me!
The southland I must seek——
Kildee!
[A Bobolink:
Link-a-link! Link-a-link!
My diet has made me weak;
The fields of rice must be so nice.
 160
[To the Kildeer:
I'll go with you, I think——
Link-a-link!
[A Red-Shouldered Blackbird:
Bobaree! Bobaree!
A frost you'll see——
You'll see to your sorrow,
If you wait until to-morrow——
Bobaree!
[A Chipping-Bird:
Chip-chip! Chip-chip! Chip-chip!
I'll give November the slip!
[A House-Wren:
Sh! Sh! Sh!
Every one loves the Wren!

46

Wait, and just once again
I'll go, and, as still as a mouse,
Peep into the little house
They built for my use alone,
With a door and a porch like their own!
—Sh!
161
[A Maryland Yellow-Throat Interrupting:
Witches here! Witches here!
And no wonder—so late in the year!
[A Flock of Wild Geese Flying Over:
On! On! On!
Why should we longer stay?
On! Ere the peep of day
We should be leagues away,
Quite out of sight of land!
Our old gray Commodore
Will guide our gallant band
With the daintiest food in store!
To a pleasant southern shore,
On! On! On!
[A Flock of Swallows Rising:
Zip! Zip! You may count on the Swallow!
We hear, and anear we will be;
The rest, if they like, may follow
O'er land and o'er sea.
[A Bluebird to Her Mate:
Weary! Oh, weary! Oh, weary!
It's a long, long, long way, dearie!
162
[A Robin:
Quip! Quip! Cheer up! Cheer up!
But I think we ought first to sup;
With such a long journey ahead,
Pilgrims should be well fed——
Quip! Quip!
[A Highlander Shouts from the Top of a Dead Tree:
A-wick-wick! wick-wick! wick-wick! wick! Yare-op!
If all this senseless chatter you would stop,
And listen, an announcement I would make:
Old Father Crane will soon be here to take
All you small folks upon his back—Wick-wick!
Chorus of Small Birds
[Chippy, Wren, Yellow-bird, Pewee, Kinglet, etc.:
Peet-weet! Zit! Zit! Cheeree! Ittee! Be Quick!
Edith M. Thomas.
163
THE KIND OLD OAK

It was almost time for winter to come. The little birds had all gone far away, for they were afraid of the cold. There was no green grass in the fields, and there were no pretty flowers in the gardens. Many of the trees had dropped all their leaves. Cold winter, with its snow and ice, was coming.

At the foot of an old oak tree, some sweet little violets were still in blossom. "Dear old oak," said they, "winter is coming: we are afraid that we shall die of the cold."

"Do not be afraid, little ones," said the oak, "close your yellow eyes in sleep, and trust to me. You have made me glad many a time with your sweetness. Now I will take care that the winter shall do you no harm."

So the violets closed their pretty eyes and went to sleep; they knew that they could trust the kind old oak. And the great tree softly 164 dropped red leaf after red leaf upon them until they were all covered over.

The cold winter came, with its snow and ice, but it could not harm the little violets. Safe under the friendly leaves of the old oak they slept, and dreamed happy dreams until the warm rains of spring came and waked them again.

"No more the summer floweret charms,
The leaves will soon be sere,
And autumn folds his jeweled arms
Around the dying year."
165
THE TREE

The tree's early leaf-buds were bursting their brown;
"Shall I take them away?" said the Frost, sweeping down.
"No, dear, leave them alone
Till the blossoms have grown,"
Prayed the tree, while it trembled from rootlet to crown.
The tree bore its blossoms, and all the birds sung:
"Shall I take them away?" said the Wind, as it swung.
"No, dear, leave them alone
Till berries here have grown,"
Said the tree, while the leaflets all quivering hung.
The tree bore its fruit in the midsummer glow:
Said the girl, "May I gather thy berries or no?"
"Yes, dear, all thou canst see;
Take them; all are for thee,"
Said the tree, while it bent its laden boughs low.
Björnstjerne Björnson.
166
COMING AND GOING

Henry Ward Beecher
There came to our fields a pair of birds that had never built a nest nor seen a winter. How beautiful was everything! The fields were full of flowers, and the grass was growing tall, and the bees were humming everywhere. Then one of the birds began singing, and the other bird said, "Who told you to sing?" And he answered, "The flowers told me, and the bees told me, and the winds and leaves told me, and the blue sky told me, and you told me to sing." Then his mate answered, "When did I tell you to sing?" And he said, "Every time you brought in tender grass for the nest, and every time your soft wings

fluttered off again for hair and feathers to line the nest." Then his mate said, "What are you singing about?" And he answered, "I am singing about everything and nothing. It is because I am so happy that I sing." 167

By and by five little speckled eggs were in the nest, and his mate said, "Is there anything in all the world as pretty as my eggs?" Then they both looked down on some people that were passing by and pitied them because they were not birds.

In a week or two, one day, when the father-bird came home, the mother-bird said, "Oh, what do you think has happened?" "What?" "One of my eggs has been peeping and moving!" Pretty soon another egg moved under her feathers, and then another and another, till five little birds were hatched! Now the father-bird sang louder and louder than ever. The mother-bird, too, wanted to sing, but she had no time, and so she turned her song into work. So hungry were these little birds that it kept both parents busy feeding them. Away each one flew. The moment the little birds heard their wings fluttering among the leaves, five yellow mouths flew open wide, so that nothing could be seen but five yellow mouths! 168

"Can anybody be happier?" said the father-bird to the mother-bird. "We will live in this tree always, for there is no sorrow here. It is a tree that always bears joy."

Soon the little birds were big enough to fly, and great was their parents' joy to see them leave the nest and sit crumpled up upon the branches. There was then a great time! The two old birds talking and chatting to make the young ones go alone! In a little time they had learned to use their wings, and they flew away and away, and found their own food, and built their own nests, and sang their own songs of joy.

Then the old birds sat silent and looked at each other, until the mother-bird said, "Why don't you sing?" And he answered, "I can't sing—I can only think and think." "What are you thinking of?" "I am thinking how everything changes: the leaves are falling off from this tree, and soon there will be no roof over our heads; the flowers are all going; last night there was a frost; almost all the birds are flown away. Something calls me, and I feel as if I would like to fly far away." 169

"Let us fly away together!"

Then they rose silently, and, lifting themselves far up in the air, they looked to the north: far away they saw the snow coming. They looked to the south: there they saw flowers and green leaves! All day they flew; and all night they flew and flew, till they found a land where there was no winter—where flowers always blossom, and birds always sing. 170

A LEGEND OF THE WILLOW TREE

(Japanese Legend Retold)
Once upon a time a humble willow tree with gnarled and twisted branches grew near a tall and stately companion called the bamboo tree. Many people who passed by stopped to admire the shapely bamboo, but no one seemed to notice the old willow tree.

One morning when the sun shone brightly after a soft rain a timid little plant with a delicate stem sprang up between the two trees, and looked pleadingly toward the straight, strong trunk of the bamboo. But the bamboo tossed her plumy foliage and said haughtily, "Do not look to me for help. I shall not let you cling around my trunk."

"Let me take hold of you until I grow a little stronger," begged the little plant. But the bamboo drew away and said, "Keep away. I can not allow you to cling to my beautiful branches." 171

Then the kind old willow tree whispered through her leaves, "Do not be discouraged, little one. The sun is shining, and the soft rain will come to refresh you.

49

Come to me if you like, and grip your little green fingers into my bark. Do not be afraid. In the shade of my branches you shall be protected. Come."

The tiny plant still looked longingly toward the handsome bamboo. But at last she crept over the grass to the old willow, and began to twine around the sheltering branches. Up, up, the slender vine climbed to the very top of the tree. There it tossed out so many lovely green shoots that the people who passed stopped to enjoy its beauty. And when the early fall days came large buds appeared on the vine.

The bamboo looked at the swelling buds and said, "I wonder what those ugly knobs on the vine mean. Perhaps she has brought some disease which may affect all the trees of the country."

The willow made no answer to the bamboo, but in her kindly way she 172 whispered to the vine, "Do not feel hurt, I know what the swelling buds mean."

There was a gentle rain at night, and in the morning the sun shone radiantly in a clear sky. The green buds which covered the vine burst forth into beautiful, sweet-scented blossoms. From crown to foot the old willow tree stood bedecked with glorious colour. The owner of the land called his friends to see the wonder. They looked in amazement at the richly coloured blossoms. Then the master called his labourers, and told them to clear a space about the willow tree.

"Cut down the bamboo tree that we may see the beauty of the vine."

"It is a very fine bamboo tree, master," said the head servant.

"Yes, it is, indeed," declared the master, "but there are many other bamboo trees equally fine, whereas no one has ever seen a vine with such a wealth of lovely blossoms."

So the labourers cut down the haughty bamboo tree, and left the willow and the flowering vine to be admired by many, many people.

173
AUTUMN FASHIONS

The Maple owned that she was tired of always wearing green,
She knew that she had grown, of late, too shabby to be seen!
The Oak and Beech and Chestnut then deplored their shabbiness,
And all, except the Hemlock sad, were wild to change their dress.
"For fashion-plate we'll take the flowers," the rustling Maple said,
"And like the Tulip I'll be clothed in splendid gold and red!"
"The cheerful Sunflower suits me best," the lightsome Beech replied;
"The Marigold my choice shall be," the Chestnut spoke with pride.
The sturdy Oak took time to think—"I hate such glaring hues;
The Gillyflower, so dark and rich, I for my model choose."
174
So every tree in all the grove, except the Hemlock sad,
According to its wish ere long in brilliant dress was clad.
And here they stayed through all the soft and bright October days;
They wished to be like flowers—indeed, they look like huge bouquets!
Edith M. Thomas.
175
POMONA'S BEST GIFT

Here stands a good old apple tree
Stand fast at root,
Bear well, at top;

50

Every little twig
Bear an apple big;
Every little bough
Bear an apple now;
Hats full, caps full;
Threescore sacks full!
Hullo, boys, hullo!
—Old English Song.
176

POMONA

In the far-off days, when the children of sunny Italy saw the hillside vineyards rich with purple grapes, and the branches of the orchards bending with the weight of luscious fruit, they clapped their hands and cried gleefully, "See Pomona's Gifts." They offered grateful thanks to the wood nymph whose thoughtful care brought the precious fruit to a bountiful harvest.

Carrying a curved knife in her right hand, the faithful Pomona glided swiftly up the hillside, and primed the low-bending vines of all rank shoots. By cutting away all withered branches, she kept her orchards green and trim, and thus helped the trees to bring forth richest fruit.

So happy was this nymph in her work that she gave no attention to the numerous suitors who hoped to win her. Many a time a madcap satyr 177 desiring to attract Pomona's attention danced in vain near her orchards. Pan played entrancingly on his reed pipes, but the nymph gave no heed to his music.

Among the many admirers of Pomona was a youth named Vertumnus, who presided over gardens and the changing seasons. How often he patiently planned to meet this charming nymph while she was tending her fruit and vines, but his advances were always met with a coy indifference which puzzled him. At last he determined to appear in various disguises in order to see if he could attract her attention, and discover if she cared for him. One day he took the form of a plowman, whip in hand, as if he had come from unyoking the tired oxen in a neighboring field. At another time he assumed the guise of a woodman carrying a pruning knife and ladder, then again he appeared in the garb of a hardy reaper carrying a basket filled with golden grain. But no matter what disguise he took—plowman, woodman, reaper, fruit-gatherer, soldier, fisherman—he failed to win any attention from the nymph, whose interest was centered on the precious orchards and vineyards. 178

One day when Pomona was carefully examining the ripening fruit an old woman leaning on a staff appeared before her and said, "Thy patient care will earn a precious harvest. Never have I seen such marvelous fruit. Tell me, fair nymph, does some strong youth help thee attend to the orchards and vineyards?"

The maiden shook her head and replied, "There is no youth who is constant enough to love the orchards and vineyards as dearly as Pomona."

But the old woman drew near to her and said, "There is one youth whose constancy can not be questioned, but thou hast scorned his advances. Many times has he told thee how gladly he would be thy helpmate, for nothing in nature delights him so much as the golden harvest of luscious fruit."

"Thou meanest Vertumnus," said the nymph. Then she added, "He is, indeed, worthy of thy praise."

Suddenly the old woman straightened her bent figure and threw off her 179 disguise. There before Pomona stood the handsome form of Vertumnus, who no longer felt any doubt about the nymph's love.

In the autumn sunshine under the trees, whose boughs were bending with the ripening fruit, Pomona and Vertumnus plighted their troth, and agreed to share in the labour of bringing to perfection the gifts of orchards and vineyards.

180

IN THE ORCHARD

O the apples rosy-red,
O the gnarled trunks grey and brown,
Heavy branchéd overhead;
O the apples rosy-red,
O the merry laughter sped,
As the fruit is showered down!
O the apples rosy-red,
O the gnarled trunks grey and brown.
George Weatherby.

181

JOHNNY APPLESEED

Josephine Scribner Gates

Once there was a man who was very, very poor. He had been a farmer, and no one raised such fine crops as he did. By and by, in some way, he lost his farm, and was left all alone.

He had always wanted to do some grand thing, something that would make many people happy, but what could he do? He had no money. All he had was a small boat.

As he trudged along one day, he saw some old sacks lying under a tree. As he looked at them he had a splendid thought. A thought that seemed to have wings, and came flying from far away. Oh, it was a beautiful thought, and seemed to be singing a little song in his heart, as he picked up the sacks and placed them in his boat, jumped in himself and floated away. 182

As he rowed down the stream, the man watched the shore with keen eyes. When he saw an apple orchard he rowed to land, tied his boat, hastened to the homes near the orchards and asked for work.

He cut wood, carried water, and did all sorts of odd chores. In payment for this work he asked for food, and what else do you suppose?

The people were so surprised at what he asked for they could hardly believe him. He asked that he might have the seeds from the apples on the ground under the trees—only the seeds.

Of course they gladly gave him such a simple thing, and as he cut the fruit the neighbour children swarmed about him.

From one place to another he went, always adding to his store of seeds.

Some generous farmers gave him also cuttings of peach, pear, and plum trees, and grape vines.

Day after day, day after day, he cut up the fruit, while the children sat at his feet, and listened to thrilling tales of what he had seen 183 in his travels. Of the Indians with their gay blankets and feathers, of their camps where they lived in the forests.

Of their dances and war paint; their many-coloured, beaded necklaces and jingling, silver chains and bracelets. Of their beady-eyed babies strapped to boards.

Of the wolves which came out at night to watch him as he sat by his fire; of the beautiful deer who ran across his patch.

He sang funny songs for the children, and taught them all sorts of games.

When it came time to go on, they begged him to stay. Never before had they been so amused, but on he went, and when his bags were full, and he had a goodly store of food, he started on to carry out the splendid thought. Oh, it was a grand thing he was going to do.

The little boat went on and on, till houses were no more to be seen. Splendid forests lined the banks here and there. Then he paused, for this was what he was seeking—a place where no one lived.

He landed and went about with a bag of seeds, and when he reached an open place in a forest, he planted seeds and cuttings of the 184 trees and vines; then wove a brush fence about them to keep the deer away. He then hastened back to his boat and drifted on.

In many, many places he landed and planted seeds, and all the orchards of the Ohio and Mississippi Valley we owe to this man.

Years after when settlers came looking for a place to live, they chose these spots where, to their great surprise, they found all sorts of trees loaded with fruit.

This man's name was John Chapman, but he was nicknamed Johnny Appleseed.

185

RED APPLE

The big Sky-man that makes the Moons,
Stuck one into our Apple tree;
I saw it when I went to Bed;
The Tree was black; the Moon was red,
And round as round could be.
To-day I went to get that Moon,
For I can climb the Apple-tree;
The Moon was gone. But in its stead
I found an Apple round and red,
And nice as nice could be.
Hamish Hendry.

186

THE THREE GOLDEN APPLES

Nathaniel Hawthorne

Did you ever hear of the golden apples that grew in the garden of the Hesperides? Ah, those were such apples as would bring a great price by the bushel if any of them could be found growing in the orchards of nowadays! But there is not, I suppose, a graft of that wonderful fruit on a single tree in the wide world. Not so much as a seed of these apples exists any longer.

And, even in the old, old, half-forgotten times, before the garden of the Hesperides was overrun with weeds, a great many people doubted whether there could be real trees that bore apples of solid gold upon their branches. All had heard of them, but nobody remembered to have 187 seen any. Children, nevertheless, used to listen openmouthed to stories of the golden apple-tree, and resolved to discover it when they should be big

53

enough. Adventurous young men, who desired to do a braver thing than any of their fellows, set out in quest of this fruit. Many of them returned no more: none of them brought back the apples. No wonder that they found it impossible to gather them! It is said that there was a dragon beneath the tree with a hundred terrible heads, fifty of which were always on the watch while the other fifty slept.

It was quite a common thing with young persons, when tired of too much peace and rest, to go in search of the garden of the Hesperides. And once the adventure was undertaken by a hero, who had enjoyed very little peace or rest since he came into the world. At the time of which I am going to speak he was wandering through the pleasant land of Italy, with a mighty club in his hand, and a bow and quiver slung across his shoulders. He was wrapt in the skin of the biggest and fiercest lion that ever had been seen, and which he himself had 188 killed; and though, on the whole, he was kind and generous and noble, there was a good deal of the lion's fierceness in his heart. As he went on his way he continually inquired whether that were the right road to the famous garden. But none of the country people knew anything about the matter, and many looked as if they would have laughed at the question if the stranger had not carried so very big a club.

So he journeyed on and on, still making the same inquiry, until at last he came to the brink of a river, where some beautiful young women sat twining wreaths of flowers.

"Can you tell me, pretty maidens," asked the stranger, "whether this is the right way to the garden of the Hesperides?"

On hearing the stranger's question, they dropped all their flowers on the grass, and gazed at him with astonishment.

"The garden of the Hesperides!" cried one. "We thought mortals had been weary of seeking it after so many disappointments. And pray, adventurous traveler, what do you want there?" 189

"A certain king, who is my cousin," replied he, "has ordered me to get him three of the golden apples."

"And do you know," asked the damsel who had first spoken, "that a terrible dragon with a hundred heads keeps watch under the golden apple-tree?"

"I know it well," answered the stranger calmly. "But from my cradle upward it has been my business, and almost my pastime, to deal with serpents and dragons."

The young women looked at his massive club, and at the shaggy lion's skin which he wore, and, likewise, at his heroic limbs and figure, and they whispered to each other that the stranger appeared to be one who might reasonably expect to perform deeds far beyond the might of others.

"Go back!" cried they all; "go back to your own home! Your mother, beholding you safe and sound, will shed tears of joy; and what can she do more should you win ever so great a victory? No matter for the golden apples! No matter for the king, your cruel cousin! We do not wish the dragon with the hundred heads to eat you up." 190

The stranger seemed to grow impatient at these remonstrances. He carelessly lifted his mighty club, and let it fall upon a rock that lay half-buried in the earth near by. With the force of that idle blow the great rock was shattered all to pieces.

"Do you not believe," said he, looking at the damsels with a smile, "that such a blow would have crushed one of the dragon's hundred heads?"

"But the dragon of the Hesperides, you know," observed one of the damsels, "has a hundred heads!"

"Nevertheless," replied the stranger, "I would rather fight two such dragons than a single hydra."

The traveler proceeded to tell how he chased a very swift stag for a twelvemonth together, without ever stopping to take breath, and had at last caught it by the antlers and carried it home alive. And he had fought with a very odd race of people, half-horses and half-men, and had put them all to death, from a sense of duty, in order that their ugly figures might never be seen any more. 191

"Do you call that a wonderful exploit?" asked one of the young maidens, with a smile. "Any clown in the country has done as much."

"Perhaps you may have heard of me before," said he modestly. "My name is Hercules."

"We have already guessed it," replied the maidens, "for your wonderful deeds are known all over the world. We do not think it strange any longer that you should set out in quest of the golden apples of the Hesperides. Come, sisters, let us crown the hero with flowers!"

Then they flung beautiful wreaths over his stately head and mighty shoulders, so that the lion's skin was almost entirely covered with roses. They took possession of his ponderous club, and so entwined it about with the brightest, softest, and most fragrant blossoms that not a finger's breadth of its oaken substance could be seen. Lastly, they joined hands and danced around him, chanting words which became poetry of their own accord, and grew into a choral song in honor of the illustrious Hercules. 192

"Dear maidens," said he, when they paused to take breath, "now that you know my name, will you not tell me how I am to reach the garden of the Hesperides?"

"We will give you the best directions we can," replied the damsels. "You must go to the seashore and find out the Old One, and compel him to inform you where the golden apples are to be found."

"The Old One!" repeated Hercules, laughing at this odd name. "And pray, who may the Old One be?"

"Why, the Old Man of the Sea, to be sure," answered one of the damsels. "You must talk with this Old Man of the Sea. He is a seafaring person, and knows all about the garden of Hesperides, for it is situated in an island, which he is often in the habit of visiting."

Hercules then asked whereabouts the Old One was most likely to be met with. When the damsels had informed him he thanked them for all their kindness.

But before he was out of hearing one of the maidens called after him.

"Keep fast hold of the Old One when you catch him!" cried she. 193

"Do not be astonished at anything that may happen. Only hold him fast, and he will tell you what you wish to know."

Hercules again thanked her, and pursued his way.

"We will crown him with the loveliest of our garlands," said they, "when he returns hither with the three golden apples after slaying the dragon with a hundred heads."

Hercules traveled constantly onward over hill and dale, and through the solitary woods.

Hastening forward without ever pausing or looking behind, he, by and by, heard the sea roaring at a distance. At this sound he increased his speed, and soon came to a beach where the great surf-waves tumbled themselves upon the hard sand in a long line of snowy foam. At one end of the beach, however, there was a pleasant spot where some green shrubbery clambered up a cliff, making its rocky face look soft and beautiful. A carpet of verdant grass, largely intermixed with sweet-smelling clover, covered the narrow space between the bottom of the cliff and the sea. And what should Hercules espy there but an old man fast asleep. 194

But was it really and truly an old man? Certainly, at first sight, it looked very like one, but on closer inspection it rather seemed to be some kind of a creature that lived in the sea. For on his legs and arms there were scales such as fishes have; he was web-footed and web-fingered, after the fashion of a duck; and his long beard, being of a greenish tinge, had more the appearance of a turf of seaweed than of an ordinary beard. Hercules, the instant he set eyes on this strange figure, was convinced that it could be no other than the Old One who was to direct him on his way.

Thanking his stars for the lucky accident of finding the old fellow asleep, Hercules stole on tiptoe toward him, and caught him by the arm and leg.

"Tell me," cried he, before the Old One was well awake, "which is the way to the garden of the Hesperides?"

The Old Man of the Sea awoke in a fright But his astonishment could hardly have been greater than that of Hercules the next moment. 195 For, all of a sudden, the Old One seemed to disappear out of his grasp, and he found himself holding a stag by the fore and hind leg! But still he kept fast hold. Then the stag disappeared, and in its stead there was a seabird, fluttering and screaming, while Hercules clutched it by the wing and claw. But the bird could not get away. Immediately afterward there was an ugly three-headed dog, which growled and barked at Hercules, and snapped fiercely at the hands by which he held him! But Hercules would not let him go. In another minute, instead of the three-headed dog, what should appear but Geryones, the six-legged man-monster, kicking at Hercules with five of his legs in order to get the remaining one at liberty! But Hercules held on. By and by no Geryones was there, but a huge snake like one of those which Hercules had strangled in his babyhood, only a hundred times as big. But Hercules was no whit disheartened, and squeezed the great snake so tightly that he soon began to hiss with pain. 196

You must understand that the Old Man of the Sea, though he generally looked so like the wave-beaten figurehead of a vessel, had the power of assuming any shape he pleased. When he found himself so roughly seized by Hercules, he had been in hopes of putting him into such surprise and terror by these magical transformations that the hero would be glad to let him go. If Hercules had relaxed his grasp, the Old One would certainly have plunged down to the very bottom of the sea.

But as Hercules held on so stubbornly, and only squeezed the Old One so much the tighter at every change of shape, and really put him to no small torture, he finally thought it best to reappear in his own figure.

"Pray what do you want with me?" cried the Old One as soon as he could take breath.

"My name is Hercules!" roared the mighty stranger, "and you will never get out of my clutch until you tell me the nearest way to the garden of the Hesperides."

When the old fellow heard who it was that had caught him, he saw with half an eye that it would be necessary to tell him everything that he wanted to know. Of course he had often heard of the fame of Hercules, 197 and of the wonderful things that he was constantly performing in various parts of the earth, and how determined he always was to accomplish whatever he undertook. He, therefore, made no more attempts to escape, but told the hero how to find the garden of the Hesperides.

"You must go on thus and thus," said the Old Man of the Sea, "till you come in sight of a very tall giant who holds the sky on his shoulders. And the giant, if he happens to be in the humour, will tell you exactly where the garden of the Hesperides lies."

Thanking the Old Man of the Sea, and begging his pardon for having squeezed him so roughly, the hero resumed his journey. He met with a great many strange adventures, which would be well worth your hearing if I had leisure to narrate them as minutely as they deserve.

Hercules continued his travels. He went to the land of Egypt, where he was taken prisoner, and would have been put to death if he had not slain the king of the country and made his escape. Passing through the deserts of Africa, and going as fast as he could, he arrived 198 at last on the shore of the great ocean. And here, unless he could walk on the crests of the billows, it seemed as if his journey must needs be at an end.

Nothing was before him save the foaming, dashing, measureless ocean. But suddenly, as he looked toward the horizon, he saw something, a great way off, which he had not seen the moment before. It gleamed very brightly, almost as you may have beheld the round, golden disk of the sun when it rises or sets over the edge of the world. It evidently drew nearer, for at every instant this wonderful object became larger and more lustrous. At length it had come so nigh that Hercules discovered it to be an immense cup or bowl made either of gold or burnished brass. How it had got afloat upon the sea is more than I can tell you. There it was at all events, rolling on the tumultuous billows, which tossed it up and down, and heaved their foamy tops against its sides, but without ever throwing their spray over the brim.

"I have seen many giants in my time," thought Hercules, "but never 199 one that would need to drink his wine, out of a cup like this."

And, true enough, what a cup it must have been! It was as large—as large—but, in short, I am afraid to say how immeasurably large it was. To speak within bounds, it was ten times larger than a great mill-wheel, and, all of metal as it was, it floated over the heaving surges more lightly than an acorn-cup adown the brook. The waves tumbled it onward until it grazed against the shore within a short distance of the spot where Hercules was standing.

As soon as this happened he knew what was to be done.

It was just as clear as daylight that this marvelous cup had been set adrift by some unseen power, and guided hitherward in order to carry Hercules across the sea on his way to the garden of the Hesperides. Accordingly, he clambered over the brim, and slid down on the inside. The waves dashed with a pleasant and ringing sound against the circumference of the hollow cup; it rocked lightly to and fro, and the motion was so soothing that it speedily rocked Hercules into an agreeable slumber. 200

His nap had probably lasted a good while, when the cup chanced to graze against a rock, and, in consequence, immediately resounded and reverberated through its golden or brazen substance a hundred times as loudly as ever you heard a church-bell. The noise awoke Hercules, who instantly started up and gazed around him, wondering whereabouts he was. He was not long in discovering that the cup had floated across a great part of the sea, and was approaching the shore of what seemed to be an island. And on that island what do you think he saw?

No, you will never guess it—not if you were to try fifty thousand times! It positively appears to me that this was the most marvelous spectacle that had ever been seen by Hercules in the whole course of his wonderful travels and adventures. It was a greater marvel than the hydra with nine heads, which kept growing twice as fast as they were cut off; greater than the six-legged man-monster; greater than anything that was ever beheld by anybody before or since the days of 201 Hercules, or than anything that remains to be beheld by travelers in all time to come. It was a giant!

But such an intolerably big giant! A giant as tall as a mountain; so vast a giant that the clouds rested about his midst like a girdle, and hung like a hoary beard from his chin, and flitted before his huge eyes so that he could neither see Hercules nor the golden cup in which he was voyaging. And, most wonderful of all, the giant held up his great hands and appeared to support the sky, which, so far as Hercules could discern through the clouds, was resting upon his head! This does really seem almost too much to believe.

Meanwhile the bright cup continued to float onward, and finally touched the strand. Just then a breeze wafted away the clouds from before the giant's visage, and Hercules beheld it, with all its enormous features—eyes each of them as big as yonder lake, a nose a mile long, and a mouth the same width.

Poor fellow! He had evidently stood there a long while. An ancient forest had been growing and decaying around his feet, and oak trees 202 of six or seven centuries old had sprung from the acorns, and forced themselves between his toes. The giant now looked down from the far height of his great eyes, and, perceiving Hercules, roared out:

"Who are you, down at my feet, there? And whence do you come in that little cup?"

"I am Hercules!" thundered back the hero. "And I am seeking for the garden of the Hesperides!"

"Ho! ho! ho!" roared the giant, in a fit of immense laughter. "That is a wise adventure, truly!"

"And why not?" cried Hercules. "Do you think I am afraid of the dragon with a hundred heads?"

Just at this time, while they were talking together, some black clouds gathered about the giant's middle and burst into a tremendous storm of thunder and lightning, causing such a pother that Hercules found it impossible to distinguish a word. Only the giant's immeasurable legs were to be seen, standing up into the obscurity of the tempest, and now and then a momentary glimpse of his whole figure 203 mantled in a volume of mist. He seemed to be speaking most of the time, but his big, deep, rough voice chimed in with the reverberations of the thunder-claps and rolled away over the hills like them.

At last the storm swept over as suddenly as it had come. And there again was the clear sky, and the weary giant holding it up, and the pleasant sunshine beaming over his vast height and illuminating it against the background of the sullen thunder-clouds. So far above the shower had been his head that not a hair of it was moistened by the raindrops.

When the giant could see Hercules still standing on the seashore, he roared out to him anew:

"I am Atlas, the mightiest giant in the world! And I hold the sky upon my head!"

"So I see," answered Hercules. "But can you show me the way to the garden of the Hesperides?"

"What do you want there?" asked the giant.

"I want three of the golden apples," shouted Hercules, "for my cousin, the king."

"There is nobody but myself," quoth the giant, "that can go to the 204 garden of the Hesperides and gather the golden apples. If it were not for this little business of holding up the sky, I would make half a dozen steps across the sea and get them for you."

"You are very kind," replied Hercules. "And cannot you rest the sky upon a mountain?"

"None of them are quite high enough," said Atlas, shaking his head. "But if you were to take your stand on the summit of that nearest one your head would be pretty nearly on a level with mine. You seem to be a fellow of some strength. What if you should take my burden on your shoulders while I do your errand for you?"

"Is the sky very heavy?" he inquired.

"Why, not particularly so at first," answered the giant, shrugging his shoulders, "but it gets to be a little burdensome after a thousand years."

"And how long a time," asked the hero, "will it take you to get the golden apples?"

"Oh, that will be done in a few moments!" cried Atlas. "I shall take ten or fifteen miles at a stride, and be at the garden and back 205 again before your shoulders begin to ache."

"Well, then," answered Hercules, "I will climb the mountain behind you, and relieve you of your burden."

The truth is, Hercules had a kind heart of his own, and considered that he should be doing the giant a favour by allowing him this opportunity for a ramble. And, besides, he thought that it would be still more for his own glory if he could boast of upholding the sky than merely to do so ordinary a thing as to conquer a dragon with a hundred heads. Accordingly, the sky was shifted from the shoulders of Atlas, and placed upon those of Hercules.

When this was safely accomplished, the first thing that the giant did was to stretch himself. Next, he slowly lifted one of his feet out of the forest, that had grown up around it, then the other. Then all at once he began to caper and leap and dance for joy at his freedom, flinging himself nobody knows how high into the air, and floundering down again with a shock that made the earth tremble. Then 206 he laughed—"ho! ho! ho!"— with a thunderous roar that was echoed from the mountains far and near. When his joy had a little subsided, he stepped into the sea—ten miles at the first stride, which brought him mid-leg deep; and ten miles at the second, when the water came just above his knees; and ten miles more at the third, by which he was immersed nearly to his waist. This was the greatest depth of the sea.

Hercules watched the giant until the gigantic shape faded entirely out of view. And now Hercules began to consider what he should do in case Atlas should be drowned in the sea, or if he were to be stung to death by the dragon with the hundred heads, which guarded the golden apples of the Hesperides. If any such misfortune were to happen, how could he ever get rid of the sky? And, by the by, its weight began already to be a little irksome to his head and shoulders.

"I really pity the poor giant," thought Hercules. "If it wearies me so much in ten minutes, how it must have wearied him in a thousand years!"

I know not how long it was before, to his unspeakable joy, he beheld 207 the huge shape of the giant, like a cloud, on the far-off edge of the sea. At his nearer approach Atlas held up his hand in which Hercules could perceive three magnificent golden apples as big as pumpkins, and all hanging from one branch.

"I am glad to see you again," shouted Hercules when the giant was within hearing. "So you have got the golden apples?"

"Certainly, certainly," answered Atlas, "and very fair apples they are. I took the finest that grew on the tree, I assure you. Ah, it is a beautiful spot, that garden of the Hesperides! Yes, and the dragon with a hundred heads is a sight worth any man's seeing. After all, you had better have gone for the apples yourself."

"No matter," replied Hercules. "You have had a pleasant ramble, and have done the business as well as I could. I heartily thank you for your trouble. And now, as I have a long way to go, and am rather in haste, and as the king, my cousin, is anxious to receive the golden apples, will you be kind enough to take the sky off my shoulders again?" 208

"Why, as to that," said the giant, chucking the golden apples into the air twenty miles high or thereabouts, and catching them as they came down—"as to that, my good friend, I consider you a little unreasonable. Cannot I carry the golden apples to the king, your cousin, much quicker than you could? As his majesty is in such a hurry to get them, I promise you to take my longest strides. And, besides, I have no fancy for burdening myself with the sky just now."

59

Here Hercules grew impatient, and gave a great shrug of his shoulders. It being now twilight, you might have seen two or three stars tumble out of their places. Everybody on earth looked upward in affright, thinking that the sky might be going to fall next.

"Oh, that will never do!" cried Giant Atlas with a great roar of laughter. "I have not let fall so many stars within the last five centuries. By the time you have stood there as long as I did you will begin to learn patience."

"What!" shouted Hercules, very wrathfully, "do you intend to make me bear this burden forever?" 209

"We will see about that one of these days," answered the giant. "At all events, you ought not to complain if you have to bear it the next hundred years, or perhaps the next thousand. I bore it a good while longer, in spite of the backache. Well, then, after a thousand years, if I happen to feel in the mood, we may possibly shift about again. Posterity will talk of you, I warrant it."

"Pish! a fig for its talk!" cried Hercules, with another hitch of his shoulders. "Just take the sky upon your head one instant, will you? I want to make a cushion of my lion's skin for the weight to rest upon. It really chafes me, and will cause unnecessary inconvenience in so many centuries as I am to stand here."

"That's no more than fair, and I'll do it," quoth the giant. "For just five minutes, then, I'll take back the sky. Only for five minutes, recollect. I have no idea of spending another thousand years as I spent the last. Variety is the spice of life, say I."

Ah, the thick-witted old rogue of a giant! He threw down the golden 210 apples, and received back the sky from the head and shoulders of Hercules upon his own, where it rightly belonged. And Hercules picked up the three golden apples that were as big or bigger than pumpkins, and straightway set out on his journey homeward, without paying the slightest heed to the thundering tones of the giant, who bellowed after him to come back. Another forest sprang up around his feet and grew ancient there, and again might be seen oak-trees of six or seven centuries old, that had waxed thus aged betwixt his enormous toes.

And there stands the giant to this day, or, at any rate, there stands a mountain as tall as he, and which bears his name; and when the thunder rumbles about its summit we may imagine it to be the voice of Giant Atlas bellowing after Hercules.

—Abridged.

211

OCTOBER—ORCHARD OF THE YEAR!

Bend thy boughs to the earth, redolent of glowing fruit! Ripened seeds shake in their pods. Apples drop in the stillest hours. Leaves begin to let go when no wind is out, and swing in long waverings to the earth, which they touch without sound, and lie looking up, till winds rake them, and heap them in fence corners. When the gales come through the trees, the yellow leaves trail, like sparks at night behind the flying engine. The woods are thinner so that we can see the leaves plainer, as we lie dreaming on the yet warm moss of the singing spring. The days are calm. The nights are tranquil. The year's work is done. She walks in gorgeous apparel, looking upon her long labour, and her serene eye saith, "It is good."

212

NOVEMBER

Trees bare and brown,
Dry leaves everywhere

Dancing up and down,
Whirling through the air.
Red-cheeked apples roasted,
Popcorn almost done,
Toes and chestnuts toasted,
That's November fun.
213
214
WOODLAND ANIMALS

No sound was in the woodlands
Save the squirrel's dropping shell
And the yellow leaves among the boughs,
Low rustling as they fell.
At last after watching and waiting,
Autumn, the beautiful came,
Stepping with sandals silver,
Decked with her mantle of flame.
215
THE PRETENDING WOODCHUCK

Carl S. Patton

Among the wild animals I have not known was a family of woodchucks who lived in a hollow log on the edge of a farm in New York State. Not that they cared much whether it was New York State or some other state. I mentioned it only that the details of this story may be verified by anyone who is inclined to doubt them. It was New York State.

Now here was a thing that distinguished this family to start with, from all other families of the neighbourhood—they lived in a hollow log. All their relatives and friends lived in the ground. I don't know how this family got started to living in the rotten log. But I do happen to know that though there were a great many warm discussions about the relative merits of a house in a log, and a house in the ground, and though many ground houses in the best locations and with all modern improvements were offered to this family, they stuck to the house in the log. 216

The house certainly did have one advantage; it had two doors. And not only that, the log was part of an old fence, and the fence ran between the garden and the cornfield. So in the summer when the garden stuff was fine, all you had to do was to walk down the hallway of the log, until you came to the left-hand door, and there you were right in the garden. But when fall came and the garden was dried up, but the corn was stacked in shocks or husked and put into the crib, all you had to do was to go down the hallway, to the door that turned to the right, and there you were in the cornfield. Quite aside from these advantages, who would live in a house with one door in it when he could just as well have one with two?

The log-house family consisted of father, mother, and four children. The youngest of these—the favourite of the family, was named Monax. His mother had heard that the scientific name for woodchuck was 217 Arctomys Monax, and being of a scientific turn of mind, she was much taken with this name. But no woodchuck in her neighbourhood had two names. So she took the last of the two and called her son Monax.

Monax had never been out in the world. He had been down to the two doors, and had looked out, but that was all. But he had been well instructed at home. He knew about

61

men, and how they would sometimes shoot at woodchucks; and about dogs, and about the corn-crib; and for a long time he had known all about garden vegetables and corn. He was certainly a promising boy, even his father and mother acknowledged it, but he had one weak point—he could not learn which was his right hand and which was his left.

In the fall Monax' father was laid up with rheumatism. He was a terrible old fellow to groan and carry on when he was sick, and his wife had to stand by him every minute. The house had to be fixed for winter, and the other children were at work on this. Saturday came and someone had to go to market. Who was there to go except Monax? So it was decided that Monax should go. 218

Mrs. Woodchuck gave him his instructions. She always gave everybody their instructions. Mr. Woodchuck was, like many of us, quite an important man, away from home. "You go out at the right-hand door," said Mrs. Woodchuck to Monax; "mind me, at the right-hand door. You go through the cornfield 'till you come to the big rock in the middle of it. Then you turn to the right again." She paused a moment, and a look of hesitancy or misgiving came into her face. "Do you really know," she said solemnly, "do you really know your right hand from your left?" "Yes," said Monax. "Hold up your right one," said his mother. Monax' mind was in a whirl. He tried to imagine himself with his back to the cornfield door, where he stood when he had his last lesson on the subject. If he could only get that clearly in his mind, he could remember which hand he held up then. But he was too excited to think. So he held up one hand; he hadn't the slightest idea which it was. "Certainly," said his mother, "certainly. Your 219 father said it was not safe to let you go, because you did not know your right hand from your left. But he under-rates you. He under-rates all the children." She spoke almost petulantly. Then her mind seemed to be relieved, and she proceeded with her instructions. "Through the cornfield," she said, "'till you come to the big rock; then you go to the right 'till you come to the edge of the field. You will see a couple of men in the cornfield. But do not be afraid of them; they are only scarecrows. Even if one of them has a gun, it is only a wooden one, and they can't hurt you. Go right ahead. At the edge of the cornfield, by the maple tree, you turn to the right again—always to the right. Then you will see the barn. Go in and look around there. Keep away from the horses and don't mind the odour. If you find a basket of corn on the barn floor, help yourself and come home. If you don't you will have to go a little farther. Just to the right of the barn a few yards—always to the right—is the corn-crib. That is where your father and I get most of the supplies for the family. You climb up into the old wagon-box that stands on the scaffolding, and jump from that into the crib. 220 Getting out is much easier and after that all you have to do is to come home. You needn't hurry especially. I sha'n't be worried about you, because there are no dogs there—the dog lives away over on the other side of the fence beyond the garage—and I know the scarecrows will not hurt you."

So Monax started out. Down the hall he went, pondering his instructions. If Mrs. Woodchuck had not gone back to tie another piece of red flannel around Mr. Woodchuck's rheumatic knee, she might have observed that Monax moved slowly, as if in deep thought. But she observed nothing, and so said nothing.

Monax was in deep thought. He was trying to decide which was his right hand and which was his left. If he could only be sure of either one of them he could guess at the other one. He had to know before he got to the first of the two doors. Why were anybody's two hands so much alike? How could anyone be sure which was which? He stopped and held up one, then the other; they looked just alike. He struck one of 221 them against the wall; then the other, they felt just alike. He couldn't stop long about it; if his mother caught him at it, she would probably suspect what was the matter with him, and his little journey into the world would be stopped before it began.

He came to the first door, and a sudden inspiration came to him. He never knew how it was, but he felt perfectly confident which was his right hand. It seemed perfectly simple, somehow. It was this one. So he turned out into the garden.

He didn't see any corn-shocks. But he was not surprised at that. His mother had said maybe they would have been hauled away by this time. He looked ahead. Yes, there was the big stone. It did look a good deal like a cement horse-block. "But then," he said to himself, "they make stone these days so that you can hardly tell it from cement." He looked for the two scarecrows. If they were there he would know he was right. And there they were. They were awfully good imitations of men. One of them was walking about just a little. As he went by them, 222 he noticed that neither of them had a gun, but he heard one of them say to the other, "Ever eat 'em?" "The young uns," said the other, "are pretty good; old ones too tough." Monax was much interested, but he was not frightened. On a page of the "Scientific American," which his mother brought home a few weeks before, he had read about the talking pictures that Mr. Edison had invented. He hadn't read of the talking scarecrows, but he had no doubt there were such. "You never can tell what these men will invent next," he said as he moved leisurely by.

At the big stone he turned—this way—he said to himself. "It is surprising how sure I am about my right hand now." He came to the edge of the field. There, just as his mother had said, was the barn. It looked more like a garage than a barn. But styles change. Anyway, there it was to the right, just as his mother had told him. "If you are sure of your direction everything else takes care of itself," he said. "The location is right."

He went into the barn. He noticed the odour; something like gasoline. 223 He looked for the horses; none there. He glanced about for the basket of corn. All he saw, instead, was a bunch of waste lying on top of a big red tank. Where the horses ought to have been was an automobile. "Probably they have changed it over from a barn to a garage since mother was here," he said; "if you are going to keep up with the times these days you can't stay in the house; you've got to get out where things are doing." It was no use to look for corn there. He had had no instructions to bring home gasoline. His mother used ammonia instead. So he took his time to look around the barn, and then moved leisurely out. Just a few yards to the right again, as his mother had said, was the corn-crib. He had never seen one before, and this one looked small to him. It looked more like a dog-house to him. But the location was right again—"always to the right," his mother said.

The old wagon box wasn't there. But at the back end of the corn-crib there was a board tacked up from the crib to the tree. That was probably one end of the scaffold that had held the wagon box. Of course they wouldn't leave the wagon box there all the fall. Probably 224 they were using it to haul corn, at that very moment, to that very crib.

Meantime Mrs. Woodchuck was growing very worried at home—for Monax had taken more time for his journey than his mother thought he would. Mr. Woodchuck's knee was very bad, and whenever he had rheumatism he was more pessimistic than usual. "I tell you," said he, "that boy will never get home. He doesn't know his right hand from his left." "I tell you he does," said Mrs. Woodchuck; "I tried him on it just before he went." "I wouldn't be surprised," Mr. Woodchuck stuck to his position, "if he had turned out that left-hand door, into the garden and had gone to the garage instead of the barn. There is one thing sure; if he tries to get corn out of that dog kennel, he will find out his mistake." Mr. Woodchuck's lack of sympathy always irritated his wife.

"Keep still," she said, "you will give me nervous prostration again if you keep saying such things."

Monax had climbed up onto the board. He paused to look around a 225 moment. Then thinking that he must not be quite so leisurely, he jumped quickly through the little window just under the roof.

Then things began to happen so fast that Monax could hardly keep track of them. For what Monax had really done was just what his father said he probably would do. He had turned to the left every time, where he ought to have turned to the right. He had gone through the garden instead of the cornfield, past the cement horse-block instead of the big stone, mistaken the garage for the barn, and now, worst luck of all, he had jumped into the dog kennel instead of into the corn-crib.

The old dog had been after the sheep and cows, and was fast asleep on the floor of his kennel. Still, he didn't propose to lie there and be jumped on by a woodchuck—not in his own kennel. And Monax—well, perhaps he wasn't surprised when, instead of landing on top of a crib of corn he fell clear to the bottom, and felt his feet touching something furry that moved. But it didn't have time to move much. Monax felt that a crisis had arrived in his career, and it was time 226 to act. He didn't wait to look for the door of the kennel; he didn't want to try any more new routes. He just rebounded off the back of the dog like a rubber ball from the pavement. Up he went, breaking the woodchuck record for the high jump, back through the window, onto the board, down to the ground quick as a flash. The dog was after him, but Monax was six feet ahead. Away he went, past the barn; the auto was just backing out; it came over Monax that it wasn't a barn after all. He dodged under the machine; the dog had to run around it; three feet more gained. He went by the big stone at full speed,—it looked more than ever to him like a cement horse-block. Past the two scarecrows; he could see that they had moved quite a little since he passed them coming out, and one of them had a gun now. Bang, it went; he felt the shot pass through his tail, and it increased his speed to forty miles. He didn't have much time to reflect, but it did come over him that those were not scarecrows, but men, and that what he had overheard them say a half hour before about the "young uns being 227 good to eat" might possibly have had some reference to himself. On he sped, through the garden; it was perfectly plain now that it had never been a cornfield, and on like a flash through the garden door into the log-house, and into his father's room—fluttering, trembling, and more dead than alive.

"Did you turn to the right?" asked his mother.

"I did—on the way back," said Monax.

228

MRS. BUNNY'S DINNER PARTY

Anna E. Skinner
Reprinted from "The Churchman."

"Are you ready, my dear?" said Mr. Bobtail, looking at his large watch. "Mrs. Bunny will expect us to come in good time to her dinner party."

"I shall be ready in a few minutes, Mr. Bobtail. I wonder how many are invited. We always meet fine people at Mrs. Bunny's house."

Mrs. Bobtail brought out her little gray silk bonnet, and Mr. Bobtail's best birch cane.

"Come," she said, "it is a good half hour's walk to Bramble Hollow. Shall we go around by the way of Cabbage-Patch Lane?"

"Oh, no, my dear, let us take a short cut through the meadow."

Off they started arm in arm across the sunlit fields.

"See, there are Mr. and Mrs. Frisk gathering nuts," said Mr. Bobtail. 229 "Jack Frost shook the trees last night. There are plenty lying on the ground."

"Good morning. How are all the little Friskies?" called Mrs. Bobtail.

"Oh, how do you do! They are quite well, thank you," said Mrs. Frisk.

"The nuts are fine this fall, Mr. Frisk," said Mr. Bobtail, shaking hands with his friend.

"Yes, indeed. We have gathered a great many for our winter store. But you see we dare not stop long in this open field." Mr. Frisk dropped his voice and glanced about in all directions. Then he added, "This is hunting season, you know."

"What! Do you mean you are afraid of hunters?" asked Mr. Bobtail in surprise.

"Indeed, we are," said Mrs. Frisk, coming a little nearer. "From our cosy home up in the hollow of this tree we saw two hunters crossing the field this morning. When their dogs sniffed about the ground and barked up the tree, we held our breath in fear."

"Yes," added Mr. Frisk, "and in a short time we heard 'bang! bang!' I 230 tell you we didn't venture down to gather nuts for several hours."

"How dreadful! And we are on our way to Mrs. Bunny's dinner party," said Mrs. Bobtail, looking in all directions; "do you think we had better go on, my dear?"

"Of course! Of course! I've never had the least fear of a gun! Let hunters bang away as much as they please, they will never frighten me." Mr. Bobtail straightened up as he spoke, and tossed back his head. "Come, Mrs. Bobtail. Good day, my friends."

"Good day. We hope you will have a pleasant time," said Mr. Frisk.

"Isn't Mr. Bobtail wonderfully brave?" said Mrs. Frisk, looking after her friends.

When they came near Bramble Hollow, Mr. and Mrs. Bobtail met some of their friends. There were Mr. and Mrs. Pinkeye, Mr. and Mrs. Longears, Mr. and Mrs. Cottontail,—all on their way to the dinner party.

Mr. and Mrs. Bunny were waiting for their guests. The little Bunnies had been told how to behave. 231

"Now, my dears," their mother had said, "you may play out-of-doors while we are at dinner. When we have finished I'll call you. Now no matter how hungry you are don't dare peep in at the windows. And if anything happens to frighten you slip into the kitchen and wait there quietly until I come."

Away scampered four happy little Bunnies.

At noon all the guests had reached Bramble Hollow. Mr. and Mrs. Bunny welcomed them, and in a little while all were seated around the table laughing and talking merrily.

"What fine salad this is, Mrs. Bunny," said Mrs. Longears. "The cabbage hearts are very sweet this fall."

Mrs. Bunny nodded pleasantly and said, "Do have some lettuce, Mr. Bobtail. I'm sure your long walk must have made you hungry."

"I hope you will like our carrots," said Mr. Bunny, helping himself to another. "Come, Mrs. Cottontail, let me help you to another serving of turnip tops." 232

"Thank you, Mr. Bunny. What a pleasant home you have here in Bramble Hollow. Do hunters ever wander into this quiet corner?"

"Well, yes. They stroll through the hollow sometimes."

"Dear me," said Mrs. Cottontail.

"Our friends, Mr. and Mrs. Frisk, were telling us that they saw two hunters crossing the fields this morning," said Mrs. Bobtail.

"This morning!" cried some of the guests, pricking up their ears.

65

"Come, come, my friends," said Mr. Bobtail, laughing, "I see I shall have to quiet you. I never could see why so many rabbits are afraid of a gun! I have often stayed quietly under a hedge while a hunter fired shots as near to me as——"

"Bang! bang! bang!"

Four little Bunnies leaped through the window, and jumped right over the table, upsetting many of the dishes.

Mr. Bobtail darted off his chair at the same time, and rushed to a corner of the kitchen, where he stayed, shaking with fear. 233

The other guests did not move or speak for several minutes. Then Mrs. Bunny caught sight of Mr. Bobtail in the corner. "Come out, Mr. Bobtail," she called, "I'm sure the hunters have gone into the next field."

234

THE NUTCRACKERS OF NUTCRACKER LODGE

Harriet Beecher Stowe

Mr. and Mrs. Nutcracker were as respectable a pair of squirrels as ever wore gray brushes over their backs. They lived in Nutcracker Lodge, a hole in a sturdy old chestnut tree overhanging a shady dell. Here they had reared many families of young Nutcrackers, who were models of good behavior in the forest.

But it happened in the course of time that they had a son named Featherhead, who was as different from all the other children of the Nutcracker family as if he had been dropped out of the moon into their nest. He was handsome enough, and had a lively disposition, but he was sulky and contrary and unreasonable. He found fault with everything his respectable papa and mama did. Instead of helping with 235 up nuts and learning other lessons proper to a young squirrel,—he sneered at all the good old ways and customs of the Nutcracker Lodge, and said they were behind the times. To be sure he was always on hand at meal times, and played a very lively tooth on the nuts which his mother had collected, always selecting the best for himself. But he seasoned his nibbling with much grumbling and discontent.

Papa Nutcracker would often lose his patience, and say something sharp to Featherhead, but Mamma Nutcracker would shed tears, and beg her darling boy to be a little more reasonable.

While his parents, brothers, and sisters were cheerfully racing up and down the branches laying up stores for the winter, Featherhead sat apart, sulking and scolding.

"Nobody understands me," he grumbled. "Nobody treats me as I deserve to be treated. Surely I was born to be something of more importance than gathering a few chestnuts and hickory-nuts for the winter. I am an unusual squirrel." 236

"Depend upon it, my dear," said Mrs. Nutcracker to her husband, "that boy is a genius."

"Fiddlestick on his genius!" said old Mr. Nutcracker; "what does he do?"

"Oh, nothing, of course, but they say that is one of the marks of genius. Remarkable people, you know, never come down to common life."

"He eats enough for any two," said old Nutcracker, "and he never helps gather nuts."

"But, my dear, Parson Too-Whit, who has talked with Featherhead, says the boy has very fine feelings,—so much above those of the common crowd."

"Feelings be hanged," snapped old Nutcracker. "When a fellow eats all the nuts that his mother gives him, and then grumbles at her, I don't believe much in his fine feelings. Why doesn't he do something? I'm going to tell my fine young gentleman that if he doesn't behave himself I'll tumble him out of the nest neck and crop, and see if hunger won't do something toward bringing down his fine airs." 237

"Oh, my dear," sobbed Mrs. Nutcracker, falling on her husband's neck with both paws, "do be patient with our darling boy."

Now although the Nutcrackers belonged to the fine old race of the Grays, they kept on the best of terms with all branches of the squirrel family. They were very friendly to the Chipmunks of Chipmunk Hollow. Young Tip Chipmunk, the oldest son, was in all respects a perfect contrast to Master Featherhead. Tip was lively and cheerful, and very alert in getting food for the family. Indeed, Mr. and Mrs. Chipmunk had very little care, but could sit at the door of their hole and chat with neighbours, quite sure that Tip would bring everything out right for them, and have plenty laid up for winter.

"What a commonplace fellow that Tip Chipmunk is," sneered Featherhead one day. "I shall take care not to associate with him."

"My dear, you are too hard on poor Tip," said Mrs. Nutcracker. "He is a very good son, I'm sure."

"Oh, I don't doubt he's good enough," said Featherhead, "but he's so common. He hasn't an idea in his skull above his nuts and Chipmunk 238 Hollow. He is good-natured enough, but, dear me, he has no manners! I hope, mother, you won't invite the Chipmunks to the Thanksgiving dinner—these family dinners are such a bore."

"But, my dear Featherhead, your father thinks a great deal of the Chipmunks—they are our relatives you know," said Mother Nutcracker.

"So are the High-Flyers our relatives. If we could get them to come there would be some sense to it. But of course a flying squirrel would never come to our house if a common chipmunk is a guest. It isn't to be expected," said Featherhead.

"Confound him for a puppy," said old Nutcracker. "I wish good, industrious sons like Tip Chipmunk were common."

But in the end Featherhead had his way, and the Chipmunks were not invited to Nutcracker Lodge for Thanksgiving dinner. However, they were not all offended. Indeed, Tip called early in the morning to pay his compliments of the season, and leave a few dainty beechnuts. 239

"He can't even see that he is not wanted here," sneered Featherhead.

At last old papa declared it was time for Featherhead to choose some business.

"What are you going to do, my boy?" he asked. "We are driving now a thriving trade in hickory nuts, and if you would like to join us——"

"Thank you," said Featherhead, "the hickory trade is too slow for me. I was never made to grub and delve in that way. In fact I have my own plans."

To be plain, Featherhead had formed a friendship with the Rats of Rat Hollow—a race of people whose honesty was doubtful. Old Longtooth Rat was a money-lender, and for a long time he had had his eye on Featherhead as a person silly enough to suit the business which was neither more nor less than downright stealing.

Near Nutcracker Lodge was a large barn filled with corn and grain, besides many bushels of hazelnuts, chestnuts and walnuts. Now old Longtooth told Featherhead that he should nibble a passage into the 240 loft, and set up a commission business there—passing out nuts and grain as Longtooth wanted them. He did not tell Featherhead a certain secret—namely, that a Scotch terrier was about to be bought to keep rats from the grain.

"How foolish such drudging fellows as Tip Chipmunk are!" said Featherhead to himself. "There he goes picking up a nut here and a grain there, whereas I step into property at once."

"I hope you are honest in your dealings, my son," said old Nutcracker.

Featherhead threw his tail saucily over one shoulder and laughed. "Certainly, sir, if honesty means getting what you can while it is going, I mean to be honest."

Very soon Featherhead seemed to be very prosperous. He had a splendid hole in the midst of a heap of chestnuts, and he seemed to be rolling in wealth. He lavished gifts on his mother and sisters; he carried his tail very proudly over his back. He was even gracious to Tip Chipmunk.

But one day as Featherhead was lolling in his hole, up came two boys 241 with the friskiest, wiriest Scotch terrier you ever saw. His eyes blazed like torches. Featherhead's heart died within him as he heard the boys say, "Now we'll see if we can catch the rascal that eats our grain."

Featherhead tried to slink out of the hole he had gnawed to come in by, but found it stopped.

"Oh, you are there, are you, Mister?" cried the boy. "Well, you don't get out, and now for a chase."

And sure enough poor Featherhead ran with terror up and down through the bundles of hay. But the barking terrier was at his heels, and the boys shouted and cheered. He was glad at last to escape through a crack, though he left half of his fine brush behind him—for Master Wasp, the terrier, made a snap at it just as Featherhead was squeezing through. Alas! all the hair was cleaned off so that it was as bare as a rat's tail.

Poor Featherhead limped off, bruised and beaten, with the dog and boys still after him, and they would have caught him if Tip 242 Chipmunk's hole had not stood open to receive him. Tip took the best of care of him, but the glory of Featherhead's tail had gone forever. From that time, though, he was a sadder and a wiser squirrel than he ever had been before.

243

BUSHY'S BRAVERY

Mr. Squirrel was disappointed when he peeped his head out of his hollow tree early one morning. Not one nut was to be seen on the ground.

"Jack Frost did not come last night. I see no nuts anywhere. It will take a long time to get all we need from the tree, I fear," he said to Mrs. Squirrel, who was standing close beside him.

"But Jack Frost will come to our tree," she said. "He never fails. See, there's Mrs. Bushytail out early. She seems to be looking around, too. Perhaps Jack Frost has shaken them down for her. Let's run down and see."

Away frisked Mr. and Mrs. Squirrel as fast as their legs could take them, to see what Jack Frost had done for their neighbour. But, no, he had not visited Mrs. Bushytail's tree. She had looked all over the ground, and there wasn't a nut in sight. She couldn't explain it herself. 244

"Let us wait until to-morrow morning," said Mrs. Squirrel, "he will be sure to come to-night. Then what fun Bushy and Frisky will have gathering them. They will have to work hard to get enough for our winter store. Boys love nuts, too," she added with a sigh. "But we will wait."

Morning came and frosty Jack had been there in earnest, for the nuts lay all over the ground.

"Now to work," said Father Squirrel. "Come, Bushy and Frisky."

It was a busy day for Mr. Squirrel's family. They well knew how many, many nuts are needed for the winter's store, and Mr. Squirrel kept telling Bushy and Frisky that they would have to work hard, and perhaps until the sun went down that day.

But alas for those little squirrels. "Boys love nuts, too," Mrs. Squirrel had said over and over again, and when a rustle was heard in the bushes behind the trees, and the sound of boys' voices came loud 245 and clear, these little workers had to take to their heels, and whisk up the hollow tree. There they stayed trembling with fear. In a few minutes Bushy, a little braver than the rest, ventured to peep out of a small hole. Frisky stood just back of him.

"Boys—three of them—and they all have bags!"

Poor Bushy and Frisky. If there was one thing that these little squirrels loved to do more than another it was to gather nuts—and now their chance was spoiled, for the boys were really there, and would be sure to take every nut they could find.

"They're working hard," said Bushy.

"Will they leave any for us?" asked Frisky, not even daring to peep out.

"Sh! Listen, Frisky. I heard one of the boys say that there are some nuts under the other tree. Two of the boys are going there now. It's Mrs. Bushytail's tree. But look, Frisky, they have left two of the bags."

"Where, Bushy?"

"One of the boys is sitting on one of them. He is cracking nuts, I think." 246

"And the other bag, Bushy?"

"The other one is close by our tree," and before any one could say a word, Bushy was out of the hole, down the tree, and close to the big bag. Mrs. Squirrel tried to call him back, but it was of no use. Up and down the bag he ran, first to the top and then to the sides. But he could not get in—the bag was tied tight. But Bushy's teeth were sharp.

"Dear, dear," said his mother, "here come the boys back, and they will surely see Bushy—dear, dear."

Bushy caught sight of the boys coming toward the tree for their bags, and with a whisk and a scamper he was up the tree again and into his hole in no time.

"Dear, dear Bushy," said his mother. "What a fright you gave us all. Just see those boys. There's no telling what would have happened if they had seen you."

Mr. Squirrel's family watched the boys pick up their bags, throw them over their shoulders and go away.

"Why, Tom, look at your bag," said one of the boys. "It has a hole in it. You must have lost ever so many nuts along the way." 247

"A hole?" asked Tom in surprise, as he lifted the bag from his shoulder. "So it has—and a pretty big one, too. I wonder how it ever came there. It wasn't there when I started."

The boys were gone, and Mr. Squirrel's family ventured out once more.

"It's of no use, I fear," began Mrs. Squirrel; "those boys were good workers and—dear me, here are nuts sprinkled all along the road. What does it mean?" asked Mrs. Squirrel.

"It is strange," said Mr. Squirrel. "I really thought those boys had found them all, but perhaps boys' eyes are not so sharp as we think."

Bushy kept on gathering the nuts and smiling to himself. How sly he was. Not one of the family seemed to guess the truth. It was only when he and Frisky were going to bed that night that Frisky dared to whisper, "Bushy, did you put that hole in that bag?"

248

NUT GATHERERS

Hark! how they chatter
Down the dusk Road,
See them come patter,
Each with his Load.
What have you sought, then,
Gay little Band?
What have you brought, then,
Each in his Hand?
No need to ask it;
No need to tell;
In Bag and in Basket
Your nuts show well!
Nuts from the wild-wood;
Sweet Nuts to eat;
Sweetest in Childhood
When life is sweet.
There they go patter,
Each with his Load;
Hark! how they chatter
Down the dusk Road.
Hamish Hendry.
249
250

IN HARVEST FIELDS

WHEN THE FROST IS ON THE PUMPKIN'

When the frost is on the punkin' and the fodder's in the shock,
And you hear the kyouck and gobble of the struttin' turkey-cock,
And the clackin' of the guiney's, and the cluckin' of the hens,
And the rooster's hallylcoyer as he tiptoes on the fence,
O, it's then's the time a feller is a-feelin' at his best,
With the risin' sun to greet him from a night of peaceful rest,
As he leaves the house, bareheaded, and goes out to feed the stock,
When the frost is on the punkin' and the fodder's in the shock.
James Whitcomb Riley.
251

ORIGIN OF INDIAN CORN

Once upon a time an Indian chief sat alone in his wigwam thinking about the needs of his tribe. For more than a year food had been very scarce, and they were suffering from a scanty fare of roots, herbs, and berries. Many of the people had come to him in their misery.

"We ask you to help us, brave chief," they cried. "Will you not entreat the Great Spirit to send us some of the food from the Happy Hunting Grounds where it is so plentiful? See how weak and thin our young braves are. Help us or we shall die."

"I'll go into the depths of the forest," said the chief. "There I'll live until the Great Spirit tells me how to relieve the misery of my people."

70

He left his wigwam and walked far into the forest, where he waited for several days before the Great Spirit spoke these words to him:
252
"In the moon of rains take thy family and go to the stretch of land which joins this forest. Wait there until I send thee a message."

The chief went back to the Indian village, and told what he had heard from the Great Spirit. And in the Moon of Rains he called together his honoured wife, his fleet-footed sons, and his graceful daughter, and said, "Follow me to the stretch of land beyond the forest."

When they reached the great plain, they stood in a group waiting for a message from the Great Spirit. For three suns they stood patiently without once changing their positions.

The Indians of the tribe grew anxious to know what had happened to their chief and his family, and some of them slipped through the wood to the plain where they knew he had been directed to go. There they saw the group of figures standing with their hands uplifted, and their eyes closed. The Indians were filled with awe.

"The Great Spirit is talking to them," they whispered, as they went back to their wigwams. 253

In a few days they returned to the plain. A marvelous sight met their eyes. Instead of the chief and his family standing like images of sleep, they saw wonderful green plants, tall and straight, with broad, flat leaves, and in place of uplifted hands they beheld ears of corn with silken fringe.

"The Great Spirit has called our chief and his family to the 'Happy Hunting Grounds,'" they said, "and has sent us this food as a symbol of their sacrifice."

They saved some of the kernels and planted them in the fields, and each year when they reaped a golden harvest they remembered the brave chief whose thoughtful care brought them the rich blessing of the Indian corn. 254

Sing, O Song of Hiawatha,
Of the happy days that followed,
In the land of the Ojibways,
In the pleasant land and peaceful!
Sing the mysteries of Mondamin,
Sing the Blessing of the Cornfields!
Henry W. Longfellow.
255
O-NA-TAH: THE SPIRIT OF THE CORN-FIELDS

Harriet Converse

O-na-tah is the spirit of the corn, and patroness of the fields. The sun touches her dusky face with the blush of the morning, and her dark eyes grow soft as the gleam of the stars that float on dark streams. Her night-black hair flares in the breeze like the wind-driven cloud that unveils the sun. As she walks the air, draped in her maize, its blossoms plume to the sun, and its fringing tassels play with the rustling leaves in whispering promises to the waiting fields. Night follows O-na-tah's dim way with dews, and Day guides the beams that leap from the sun to her path. And the great Mother Earth loves O-na-tah, who brings to her children their life-giving grain. 256

At one time O-na-tah had two companions, the Spirit of the Bean and the Spirit of the Squash. In the olden time when the bean, corn, and squash were planted together in the hill these three plant spirits were never separated. Each was clothed in the plant which she guarded. The Spirit of the Squash was crowned with the flaunting gold trumpet blossom of its foliage. The Spirit of the Bean was arrayed in the clinging leaves of its winding vine, its velvety pods swinging to the breeze.

One day when O-na-tah had wandered astray in search of the lost dew, Hah-gweh-da-et-gab captured her, and imprisoned her in his darkness under the earth. Then he sent one of his monsters to blight her fields and the Spirit of Squash and the Spirit of Bean fled before the blighting winds that pursued them. O-na-tah languished in the darkness, lamenting her lost fields. But one day a searching sun ray discovered her, and guided her safely back to her lands.

Sad indeed was O-na-tah when she beheld the desolation of her 257 blighted fields, and the desertion of her companions, Spirit of Squash and Spirit of Bean. Bewailing the great change, she made a vow that she would never leave her fields again.

If her fields thirst now, she can not leave them to summon the dews. When the Flame Spirit of the Sun burns the maize O-na-tah dare not search the skies for Ga-oh to implore him to unleash the winds and fan her lands. When great rains fall and blight her fields the voice of O-na-tah grows faint and the Sun can not hear. Yet faithful she watches and guards, never abandoning her fields till the maize is ripe.

When the maize stalk bends low O-na-tah is folding the husks to the pearly grains that the dew will nourish in their screening shade, as they fringe to the sun.

When the tassels plume, O-na-tah is crowning the maize with her triumph sign, and the rustling leaves spear to the harvest breeze.

258

MONDAMIN

Summer passed and Shawondasee
Breathed his sighs o'er all the landscape,
From the South-land sent his ardours,
Wafted kisses warm and tender;
And the maize-field grew and ripened,
Till it stood in all the splendour
Of its garments green and yellow,
Of its tassels and its plumage,
And the maize-ears full of shining
Gleamed from bursting sheaths of verdure.
Then Nokomis, the old woman,
Spake, and said to Minnehaha,
"'Tis the Moon when leaves are falling,
All the wild rice has been gathered,
And the maize is ripe and ready;
Let us gather in the harvest,
Let us wrestle with Mondamin,
Strip him of his plumes and tassels,
Of his garments green and yellow."
And the merry Laughing Water
Went rejoicing from the wigwam,
With Nokomis, old and wrinkled,
And they called the women round them,
Called the young men and the maidens,
To the harvest of the cornfields,

To the husking of the maize-ear.

Henry W. Longfellow.

259

THE DISCONTENTED PUMPKIN

Jack Frost visited Farmer Crane's field one night, and the next morning the gold of the pumpkins shone more brilliantly than ever through their silver coverings.

"It is of no use," said one large pumpkin to another lying beside it. "It is of no use. I was never made to be cut up for pumpkin pies. I feel I was put here for something higher."

"Why, what do you mean?" said the other. "You never seemed dissatisfied before. You quite take my breath away."

"Well, to tell the truth, I do not like the thought of being cut up and served on a table like an ordinary pumpkin. See how large I am, and what a glorious colour. Tell me, did you ever see a pumpkin more beautiful?"

"You are beautiful, indeed, but I never thought of being made for anything but pies. Do tell me of what other use can one be?" 260

"Well, I have always thought that I am not like the other pumpkins in this field, and when Farmer Crane pointed me out as the finest one he had, I heard him say, 'That would be a fine one for a fair.' It was not till then that I really knew for what I was intended."

"I do remember," answered the other. "Yes, I do remember hearing about some pumpkins' being taken to a county fair once, but I never heard how they liked it. As for myself, I should be proud to be made into delicious pies and served on a beautiful plate."

"How can you be satisfied with that thought? But there is Farmer Crane now. He is gathering some of the smaller pumpkins to make pies with, I think."

"Perhaps he knows best what you are made for," answered the other.

Farmer Crane was soon at their side, and was looking from one to the other.

"What fine pies they will make. I had better take them now, I think," he said, and they were quickly added to the golden heap already on the wagon. 261

How happy they all were—all but one that lay on the top of the large pile.

"It is hard to be thrown in with these ordinary pumpkins. If I could only slip off by myself. Perhaps there is at least a place at the bottom of the wagon where I can be alone."

It was a long way from the top of the pile to the bed of the wagon, but it was very little trouble to slip away from the rest. It would take only a second, and then he could be away from the others. But alas! the discontented pumpkin slipped a little too far, and I'm sorry to say, soon lay on the frozen ground, a shattered heap.

"Dear me," said the pumpkins in one breath; "see, that fine fellow has slipped off, and is broken to pieces. What a feast the cows and pigs will have."

"It is too bad," said one.

"And he was so anxious to be taken to a fair," added another. 262

Hurrah for the tiny seed!
Hurrah for the flower and vine!
Hurrah for the golden pumpkin;
Yellow and plump and fine!
But better than all beginnings,
Sure, nobody can deny,
Is the end of the whole procession——
This glorious pumpkin pie!

263
BOB WHITE

I see you on the zig zag rails,
You cheery little fellow!
While purple leaves are whirling down,
And scarlet, brown or yellow.
I hear you when the air is full
Of snow-down of the thistle;
All in your speckled jacket trim,
"Bob White! Bob White!" you whistle.
Tall amber sheaves, in rustling rows,
Are nodded there to greet you,
I know that you are out for play——
How I should like to meet you!
Though blithe of voice, so shy you are,
In this delightful weather;
What splendid playmates, you and I,
Bob White, would make together.
There, you are gone! but far away
I hear your whistle falling,
Ah! maybe it is hide and seek,
And that's why you are calling.
Along those hazy uplands wide
We'd be such merry rangers;
What! silent now and hidden, too?
Bob White, don't let's be strangers.
264
Perhaps you teach your brood the game,
In yonder rainbowed thicket,
While winds are playing with the leaves,
And softly creaks the cricket.
"Bob White! Bob White!" again I hear
That blithely whistled chorus,
Why should we not companions be?
One Father watches o'er us!
George Cooper.
265
THE LITTLE PUMPKIN

Emma Florence Bush.
Once there was a little pumpkin that grew on a vine in a field. All day long the sun shone on him, and the wind blew gently around him. Sometimes the welcome rain fell softly upon him, and as the vine sent her roots deep down into the earth and drew the good sustenance from it, and it flowed through her veins, the little pumpkin drank greedily of the good juice, and grew bigger and bigger, and rounder and rounder, and firmer and firmer.

By and by he grew so big he understood all that the growing things around him were saying, and he listened eagerly.

"I came from the seed of a Jack-o'-lantern," said this vine to a neighbour, "therefore I must grow all Jack-o'-lanterns." 266

"So did I," said a neighbour, "but no Jack-o'-lanterns for me. It is too hard a life. I am going to grow just plain pumpkins."

When the little pumpkin heard he was supposed to be a Jack-o'-lantern, he grew very worried, for he could not see that he was in any way different from any ordinary pumpkin, and if Mother Vine expected him to be a Jack-o'-lantern, he did not want to disappoint her.

At last he grew so unhappy over it that the dancing little sunbeams noticed it. "What is the matter, little pumpkin?" they cried. "Why do you not hold up your head and look around as you used to do?"

"Because," answered the little pumpkin, sadly, "I have to be a Jack-o'-lantern, and I don't know how. All I know about is how to be a little yellow pumpkin."

Then the merry little breezes laughed and laughed until they shook the vine so that all the pumpkins had to tighten their hold not to be shaken off. "Oh, little pumpkin!" they cried, "why worry about what you will have to do later? Just try with all your might to be a little yellow pumpkin, and believe that if you do the best you can, 267 everything will be all right. We know a secret, a beautiful secret, and some day we will tell it to you."

"Oh, tell me now!" cried the little pumpkin, but the sunbeams and breezes laughed together, and chuckled,

"Oh no, oh no, oh no!
Just grow and grow and grow,
And some day you will know."

The little pumpkin felt comforted. "After all," he thought, "perhaps if I cannot be a Jack-o'-lantern I can be a good pumpkin, and I am so far down on the vine perhaps Mother Vine won't notice me." He looked around, and saw that all his brothers and sisters were only little pumpkins, too.

"Oh, dear," he cried, "are we going to disappoint Mother Vine? Aren't any of us going to be Jack-o'-lanterns?" Then all his little brothers and sisters laughed, and said, "What do we care about being Jack-o'-lanterns? All we care about is to eat the good juice, and grow and grow." 268

At last came the cold weather, and all the little pumpkins were now big ones, and a beautiful golden yellow. The biggest and yellowest of all was the little pumpkin who had tried so hard all summer to grow into a Jack-o'-lantern. He could not believe Mother Vine did not see him now, for he had grown so big that every one who saw him exclaimed about him, and Mother Vine did not seem at all disappointed, she just kept at work carrying the good food that kept her pumpkin children well fed.

At last one frosty morning, a crowd of children came to the field. "The pumpkins are ready," they cried. "The pumpkins are ready; and we are going to find the biggest and yellowest and nicest to make a Jack-o'-lantern for the Thanksgiving party. All the grandmothers and grandfathers and aunts and uncles will see it, and we are going to eat the pies made from it."

They looked here and there, all over the field, and pushed aside the vines to see better. All at once they saw the little pumpkin. "Oh!" they cried, "What a perfect Jack-o'-lantern! So big and firm and 269 round and yellow! This shall be the Jack-o'-lantern for our Thanksgiving party, and it is so large there will be pie enough for every one."

Then they picked the pumpkin and carried him to the barn. Father cut a hole in the top around the stem, lifted it off carefully and scooped out the inside, and the children carried it to mother in the kitchen. Then father made eyes and a nose and mouth, and fitted a big candle inside. "Oh, see the beautiful Jack-o'-lantern!" they cried.

The little pumpkin waited in the barn. "At last I am a Jack-o'-lantern," he said. After a time it grew dark, and father came and carried him into the house, and lighted the candle, and put him right in the middle of the table, and all the grandmothers and grandfathers, and aunts and uncles, cried, "Oh, what a beautiful, big, round, yellow Jack-o'-lantern!"

Then the little pumpkin was happy, for he knew Mother Vine would have been proud of him, and he shone—shone—SHONE, until the candle was all burned out.

270

AUTUMN

Then came the Autumn all in yellow clad,
As though he joyèd in his plenteous store,
Laden with fruits that made him laugh, full glad
That he had banished hunger, which to-fore
Had by the body oft him pinchèd sore:
Upon his head a wreath, that was enroll'd
With ears of corn of every sort, he bore;
And in his hand a sickle he did hold,
To reap the ripen'd fruits the which the earth had yold.
Edmund Spenser.

271

272

CHEERFUL CHIRPERS

THE NEWS

The katydids say it as plain as can be
And the crickets are singing it under the trees;
In the asters' blue eyes you may read the same hint,
Just as clearly as if you had seen it in print.
And the corn sighs it, too, as it waves in the sun,
That autumn is here and summer is done.
Persis Gardiner.

273

HOW THERE CAME TO BE A KATY-DID

Patten Beard
From "The Bluebird's Garden." Used by special permission of the author and the Pilgrim Press.

Long, long, long ago—so long that this story has had time to grow into a garden legend—two green grasshoppers went out, one fine day, to play with a cricket. They played tag, and I'm on gypsyland. At last they decided to have a game of hide-and-seek.

The goal was a blade of grass, and they counted out to see who should be goal man. It fell to the little cricket, Katy-did. She was to hide her eyes behind the grassblade, and count up to one hundred by tens, while the two grasshoppers went off to hide.

So the cricket hid her face so that she could not see, and began: "Ten, twenty, thirty, forty, fifty, sixty, seventy, eighty, ninety, one hundred! Coming!" 274

76

Though there were plenty of good places in which to hide in the garden, one green grasshopper had been slow to suit himself. He had not yet hidden when the little cricket turned about and caught him.

And he began, "You didn't count up to a hundred! I didn't have time to hide! You should have hollered, 'Coming!' It's no fair! I'm not going to play any more—you didn't count up to a hundred!"

At this, the other grasshopper came out of hiding. "She did count up to a hundred," he said, "Katy did!"

She didn't"

She did!"

She didn't!"

Katy did, did, did!"

Katy didn't, didn't, didn't!"

Did, did, did!"

Didn't, didn't, didn't!"

Katy did!"

Katy didn't!"

She did!"

She didn't!"

Katy did!"

Katy didn't!"

275

To this very, very day, you can hear the dispute still going on in the garden, and the game of tag has never yet been finished. Ever since that time the grasshoppers who started the discussion have been called katydids, and the whole garden is full of the controversy. You can hear hundreds of little voices keeping it up, though nothing is ever decided. So it goes on eternally, Katy did—Katy didn't, did, did, did, didn't, didn't, she did, she didn't—for nobody has ever yet settled a dispute by contradiction. By this time, too, everyone has forgotten what the quarrel was about.

276

OLD DAME CRICKET

Old Dame Cricket, down in a thicket,
Brought up her children nine,——
Queer little chaps, in glossy black caps
And brown little suits so fine.
"My children," she said,
"The birds are abed:
Go and make the dark earth glad!
Chirp while you can!"
And then she began,——
Till, oh, what a concert they had!
They hopped with delight,
They chirped all night,
Singing, "Cheer up! cheer up! cheer!"
Old Dame Cricket,
Down in the thicket,
Sat awake till dawn to hear.
"Nice children," she said,

"And very well bred.
My darlings have done their best.
Their naps they must take:
The birds are awake;
And they can sing all the rest."
 277
MISS KATY-DID AND MISS CRICKET

Harriet Beecher Stowe
Miss Katy-Did sat on the branch of a flowering azalia in her best suit of fine green and silver, with wings of point-lace from mother nature's finest web.

Her gallant cousin, Colonel Katy-Did, had looked in to make her a morning call.

"Certainly I am a pretty creature," she said to herself when the gallant Colonel said something about being dazzled by her beauty.

"The fact is, my dear Colonel," said Miss Katy, "I am thinking of giving a party, and you must help me make out the lists."

"My dear, you make me the happiest of Katy-Dids."

"Now," said Miss Katy, drawing an azalia leaf towards her, "let us see—whom shall we have? The Fireflies are a little unsteady, but they are so brilliant, everybody wants them—and they belong to the higher circles." 278

"Yes, we must have the Fireflies," said the colonel.

"Well, then—and the Butterflies and the Moths, now there's the trouble. There are so many Moths, and they're so dull. Still if you have the Butterflies you can't leave out the Moths."

"Old Mrs. Moth has been ill lately. That may keep two or three of the Misses Moth at home," said the colonel.

"I thought she was never sick," said Miss Katy-Did.

"Yes, I understand she and her family ate up a whole fur cape last month, and it disagreed with them."

"Oh, how can they eat such things as worsted and fur?" then sneered Miss Katy-Did.

"By your fairy-like delicacy one can see that you couldn't eat such things," smiled the colonel.

"Mamma says she doesn't know what keeps me alive. Half a dewdrop and a little bit of the nicest part of a rose-leaf often lasts me for a 279 day. But to our list. Let's see,— the Fireflies, Butterflies, Moths. The Bees must come, I suppose."

"The Bees are a worthy family," nodded the colonel.

"Yes, but dreadfully humdrum. They never talk about anything but honey and housekeeping."

"Then there are the Bumble Bees."

"Oh, I dote on them," said Miss Katy-Did. "General Bumble is one of the most dashing, brilliant fellows of the day."

"He's shockingly fat!" said the colonel.

"Yes, he is a little stout," nodded Miss Katy-Did, "but he is very elegant in his manners,—something soldierly and breezy about him."

"If you invite the Bumble Bees, you must have the Hornets."

"Ah, they are spiteful,—I detest them."

"Nevertheless, one must not offend the Hornets, and how about the Mosquitoes?" asked the Colonel.

"They are very common. Can't one cut them?" 280

"I think not, my dear Miss Katy. Young Mosquito is connected with some of our leading papers, and he carries a sharp pen. It will never do to offend him."

"And I suppose one must ask all his dreadful relations, too," sighed Miss Katy.

At this moment they saw Miss Keziah Cricket coming. She carried her workbag on her arm, and she asked for a subscription to help a poor family of Ants who had just had their house hoed up by some one who was clearing the garden walks.

"How stupid of the Ants," said Katy, "not to know better than to put their house in a garden-walk."

"Ah, they are in great trouble," said Miss Cricket. "Their stores are all destroyed, and their father killed—cut quite in two by a hoe."

"How very shocking! I don't like to hear such disagreeable things. But I have nothing to give. Mamma said yesterday she didn't know how our bills were to be paid,—and there's my green satin with point lace yet to come home," said Miss Katy, shrugging her shoulders. 281

Little Miss Cricket hopped briskly off. "Poor, extravagant little thing," she said to herself.

"Shall you invite the Crickets?" said Colonel Katy-Did.

"Why, Colonel, what a question! I invite the Crickets? No, indeed."

"And shall you ask the Locusts or the Grasshoppers?"

"Certainly. The Locusts, of course—a very old and fine family, and the Grasshoppers are pretty well, and ought to be asked. But one must draw the line somewhere—and the Crickets! Why, I can't think of them."

"I thought they were very nice, respectable people," said the colonel.

"Oh, perfectly nice and respectable,—but———"

"Do explain, my dear Katy."

"Why, their colour, to be sure. Don't you see?"

"Oh!" said the colonel. "That's it, is it? And tell me, please, who decides what colour shall be the reigning colour?"

"What a question! The only true colour—the only proper one—is our 282 colour to be sure. A lovely pea green is the shade on which to found an aristocratic distinction. Of course, we are liberal; we associate with the Moths, who are gray; with the Butterflies, who are blue and gold coloured; with the Grasshoppers, yellow and brown; and society would become dreadfully mixed if it were not fortunately ordered that the Crickets are as black as jet. The fact is that a class to be looked down upon is necessary to all elegant society, and if the Crickets were not black we could not keep them down. Everybody knows they are often a great deal cleverer than we are. They have a vast talent for music and dancing; they are very quick at learning, and would be getting to the very top of the ladder if we allowed them to climb. Now, so long as we are green and they are black, we have a superiority that can never be taken from us. Don't you see now?"

"Oh, yes, I see exactly," said the colonel. "Now that Keziah Cricket, who just came in here, is quite a musician, and her old father plays the violin beautifully; by the way, we might engage him for our orchestra." 283

And so Miss Katy's ball came off. It lasted from sundown till daybreak, so that it seemed as if every leaf in the forest were alive. The Katy-Dids, and the Mosquitoes, and the Locusts, and a full orchestra of Crickets made the air perfectly vibrate.

Old Parson Too-Whit was shocked at the gaieties, which were kept up by the pleasure-loving Katy-Dids night after night.

But about the first of September the celebrated Jack Frost epidemic broke out. Poor Miss Katy, with her flimsy green satin, and point lace, was one of the first victims, and fell from the bough in company with a sad shower of last year's leaves.

The worthy Cricket family, however, avoided Jack Frost by moving in time to the chimney corner of a nice little cottage that had been built in the wood. There good old Mr. and Mrs. Cricket, with sprightly Miss Keziah and her brothers and sisters, found a warm and welcome home. When the storm howled without, and lashed the poor, naked trees, the crickets on the warm hearth would chirp out cheery welcome to the happy family in the cottage.

(Adapted.)

284

THE CRICKET

Little cricket, full of mirth,
Chirping on my kitchen hearth;
Wheresoever be thine abode,
Always harbinger of good.
Pay me for thy warm retreat
With a song more soft and sweet;
In return thou shalt receive
Such a strain as I can give.
William Cowper.

285

286

ALL HALLOWE'EN

SHADOW MARCH

Used by special permission of Charles Scribner and Sons.

All around the house is the jet black night,
It stares through the window-pane,
It creeps in the corners hiding from the light
And it moves with the moving flame.
Now my little heart goes a-beating like a drum,
With the breath of the bogie in my hair,
While all around the candle the crooked shadows come
And go marching along up the stair.
The shadow of the baluster, the shadow of the light,
The shadow of the child that goes to bed,
All the wicked shadows come a tramp, tramp, tramp,
With the black night overhead.
Robert Louis Stevenson.

287

TWINKLING FEET'S HALLOWE'EN

One Hallowe'en a band of merry pixies were dancing round and round a bright green ring in the meadow. In the center stood the Little Fiddler, playing his gayest music, and keeping time with his head and one tiny foot. The faster he played, the merrier the little creatures danced. What sport it was to twirl and twist in time with the fairy music, which the jolly little elf brought out from his tiny instrument. No wonder the pixies laughed until their sides ached. And so, indeed, did their little musician. Sometimes he was obliged to stop playing for a few seconds in order to catch his breath.

Now there was one pixie named Twinkling Feet who was the best dancer in the ring, and he could cut such queer little capers that his 288 companions fairly shrieked with laughter when they looked at him. Suddenly he thought what sport it would be to play a trick on all the little dancers. Very slyly he tripped his partner, and the two fell down in the grass, dragging with them one pixie after another until all in the circle were sprawling on the ground. There they lay for several seconds, a wriggling mass of green coats and red caps. It was some time before they could pick themselves up. Many of them laughed heartily at the mishap, but a few were so badly bruised that they were obliged to slip away and bathe their shins in the evening dew.

"Who tripped first in the ring?"

"Who made us fall on our stumjackets?"

"Who spoiled our Hallowe'en dance?" asked one little pixie after another.

"Twinkling Feet and I fell first," said the best dancer's partner. "I don't know what made us tangle our feet, do you?" he asked, laughing and turning to his companion.

But Twinkling Feet's little brown face was so drawn and sober that his partner asked quickly, "Why, what is the matter with you?"

"I don't know," said the little elf. 289

"Why, do look at him," cried another pixie.

"Does anything hurt you?" asked several little creatures together.

"I feel very queer," said Twinkling Feet.

"Have you what mortals call 'pain?'" asked his partner.

"I don't know what that is, but I feel very, very queer. Please ask the Little Fiddler if he knows what is the matter with me."

The group of pixies that had gathered around Twinkling Feet moved away in order to let the elfin musician come close to the queer-looking pixie. The little Fiddler gazed steadily at him, shook his white head, and said slowly, "A frightful thing has happened. Twinkling Feet has lost his laugh!"

"Lost his laugh!" shrieked all the other little elfs.

"He has lost his laugh!" repeated the Fiddler Pixie.

"Lost my laugh," moaned Twinkling Feet. "Oh, please tell me what to do."

"There is nothing to do but go and search for it. You can not dance 290 in a pixie ring without your laugh, and mark what I say, you must find it before midnight."

"But what if I can't find it?" cried the frightened elf.

"Then you'll be a pixie without a laugh—that is all," declared the Little Fiddler.

At these awful words every pixie's face grew sober. They looked at each other very solemnly and said, "A pixie without a laugh! How terrible!"

Then one after another they cried out. "Search for it, Twinkling Feet. Perhaps you'll find it before midnight. Start now. Think how sad it will be if you are never able to dance in the ring again."

"Where shall I go, Fiddler Pixie?" asked Twinkling Feet.

"Well, you might ask Jack-o'-Lantern," said the musician. "He's been flitting about in the meadow all the evening. See, there he goes over by the brook."

Away ran the little pixie as fast as his legs could carry him. It was no easy matter to come close enough to Jack-o'-Lantern to make him 291 hear. Twinkling Feet was almost ready to give up the chase when the little man stopped, poked his head out of his lantern, and called, "Do you wish to speak to me?"

"Don't you know me?" cried the pixie. "I'm Twinkling Feet."

"Why, what has happened to you?" asked Jack. "You're the queerest looking chap I ever saw."

"I've lost my laugh. Please tell me, Jack-o'-Lantern, have you seen it?"

"Lost your laugh!" repeated the lantern man, looking very serious. "No wonder I didn't know you. I'm very sorry to say I've seen nothing of your laugh."

"Do you know anyone who could help me, Jack?" asked Twinkling Feet. "Oh do help me find it."

"Well, let me see. You might ask Jolly Little Witch. Her eyes are very sharp. She's in the ragweed meadow, looking for a good riding stalk. As soon as she finds one I'm going to light her to the village where she will make plenty of merriment at the children's party. It's Hallowe'en, you know. Come, jump into my lantern, and I'll take you to her." 292

Twinkling Feet hopped into the little lantern, and away they went to the ragweed field. When they drew near the Jolly Little Witch called out, "I've found a good ragweed stalk, Jack, but I've lost my goggles. Come, perhaps you can help me find them. I can't go to the village without my goggles. Why, who is that in the lantern with you?"

"A pixie who wants to ask you something," said Jack-o'-Lantern, opening the door to let Twinkling Feet out. Then the lantern man hurried away to search for the witch's goggles.

"Please, Jolly Little Witch, I've lost my laugh," said Twinkling Feet.

"Lost your laugh! and on Hallowe'en! Well, no wonder I didn't know you. You're the queerest looking pixie I ever saw. Tell me how you happened to lose your laugh?"

But Twinkling Feet did not answer her question. He said meekly, "Have you seen it?"

"No, my little fellow. I'm sorry to say I've not seen your laugh," said the Jolly Little Witch. 293

"A pixie can't dance without his laugh," sighed Twinkling Feet.

"No, of course he can't. Dear, dear! How sorry I am for you," said the little witch, shaking her head.

"And if a pixie loses anything on Hallowe'en, he must find it before midnight or give it up forever."

"I could have helped you on any other night, but you see I always spend Hallowe'en in the village with the children. I shall be late to-night if I don't find those goggles." And again she began to search for them.

The pixie looked at her for a moment. Then he asked, "Do the children laugh a good deal on Hallowe'en?"

"Why, my little man, it's the time in all the year when they laugh most. To-night there is to be a witch's party. I shall secretly join the children, and play all sorts of tricks for their amusement. What a nuisance it is that I've lost those goggles."

"I'll help you search for them, Jolly Little Witch," said the pixie. 294 "I suppose I must give up my laugh, for I don't know anyone else to ask about it. Please tell me what your goggles look like."

"They are two round glass windows, which I wear over my eyes when I ride through the air," said the little Witch.

Away started the pixie to search for them. He looked carefully around every ragweed stalk in the meadow, but he could see nothing which looked like "two round glass windows."

"Perhaps one cannot find anything which has been lost on Hallowe'en," he said to himself.

Slowly he walked back to the place where he had left the Jolly Little Witch. When he reached her he stared sharply at something on top of her head.

"Please tell me more about your goggles," said Twinkling Feet. "Are they like the two glass windows across the front of your hat?"

"Across the front of my hat!" exclaimed the witch, putting her hands up to find out what the little elf meant. Then she burst out laughing, and said, "Well, well! What strange things do happen on 295 Hallowe'en! Come, Jack-o'-Lantern! Come! The pixie has found my goggles. They were on top of my head all the time!"

And turning to Twinkling Feet she said, "You shall go with us to the village, and see the merriment if you like. I'm sure Jack will carry you in his lantern."

"Of course I will," said the lantern man. "And while you are playing tricks at the children's party, I'll carry him anywhere he wishes to go. It is a long while before midnight."

"I want to see the children, and hear them laugh," said Twinkling Feet.

The Jolly Little Witch pulled her goggles down on her nose, and mounted her ragweed stalk. The pixie hopped into the lantern, and away through the air the three sailed.

When they drew near the village, the little Witch lowered herself to the ground.

"Meet me here before the party is over, Jack-o'-Lantern," she said. "I shall leave before the children take off their masks. In the meantime, let Twinkling Feet see the fun the children will have on the way to the party." 296

Away she ran up the village street to a corner where she joined a group of jolly little boys and girls on their way to the party. They wore black dresses, high, pointed hats with narrow brims, and funny little masks. Not a word did anyone speak, but the sound of their merry laughter reached Twinkling Feet's ears.

He slipped out of the lantern, and ran toward the group of children as fast as he could go. Before he reached them, however, the tiniest bit of a creature, turning somersaults faster than anyone could count, came bounding to him. It climbed up the pixie's little body, and disappeared into his mouth. Twinkling Feet burst into the merriest laugh, and ran back to Jack-o'-Lantern, crying out, "I've found it! I've found my laugh! My dear little laugh! Oh, how happy I am! Jack-o'-Lantern, please take me back to the pixie ring. I've found my dear little laugh!"

He hopped into the little man's lantern, and away over the fields they flew. As they drew near the green ring where the pixies were still dancing, the delighted elf called out, "I've found my laugh! I've found my dear little laugh!" 297

"Welcome back, Twinkling Feet," answered the dancers.

He hopped out of the lantern, and joined the other merry pixies. When they stopped dancing for a little while, the Fiddler Pixie slipped up to the Twinkling Feet, and whispered slyly, "Always watch your laugh carefully while you are dancing."

—Cornish Legend, Adapted.

298
JACK-O'-LANTERN

Here comes a Jack-o'-lantern
To frighten you to-night;
Made from a hollow pumpkin
With a candle for its light.

Go off! You Jack-o'-lantern!
You can not frighten me,
You're nothing but a pumpkin
As any one can see!
299
THE ELFIN KNIGHT

The autumn wind blew sharp and shrill around the turrets of a grey stone castle. But indoors the fire crackled merrily in my lady's bower where an old nurse was telling a tale of Elfland to Janet, the fairest of Scotch maidens.

When the story was finished, Janet's merry laugh echoed through the halls. The old nurse nodded her head earnestly and said, "'Tis well known, my lassie, that the people of Elfland revel in the hills and hollows of Scotland. Come close, and I'll tell you a secret."

Janet leaned forward, and the old woman whispered, "An Elfin Knight, named Tam Lin, haunts the moorland on the border of your father's estate. No maiden dares venture near the enchanted place, for if she should fall under the spell of this Elfin Knight she would be obliged to give him a precious jewel for a ransom." 300

"One glimpse of the Elfin Knight would be worth the rarest gem I have," laughed Janet. "How I wish I could see him!"

"Hush-sh!" said her nurse tremblingly. "Nay, nay, my lady! Mortals should have nothing to do with the people of Elfland. By all means shun the moorland at this time of the year, for to-morrow is Hallowe'en—the night when the fairies ride abroad."

But the next morning Janet bound her golden braids about her head, kilted up her green kirtle, and tripped lightly to the enchanted moorland. When she came near she saw lovely flowers blooming as gaily as if it were mid-summer time. She stooped to gather some of the roses when suddenly she heard the faintest silvery music. She glanced around, and there, riding toward her, was the handsomest knight she had ever seen. His milk-white steed, which sped along lighter than the wind, was shod in silver shoes, and from the bridle hung tiny silver bells. 301

When the knight came near, he sprang lightly from his horse and said, "Fair Janet, tell me why you pluck roses in Elfland?"

The maiden's heart beat very fast, and the flowers dropped from her hands, but she answered proudly, "I came to see Tam Lin, the Elfin Knight."

"He stands before you," said the knight. "Have you come to free him from Elfland?"

At these words Janet's courage failed, for she feared he might cast a spell over her. But when the knight saw how she trembled, he said, "Have no fear, Lady Janet, and you shall hear my story. I am the son of noble parents. One day, when I was a lad of nine years, I went hunting with my father. Now it chanced that we became separated from each other, and ill-luck attended me. My good horse stumbled, and threw me to the ground where I lay stunned by the fall. There the Fairy Queen found me, and carried me off to yonder green hill. And while it is pleasant enough in fairyland, yet I long to live among mortals again."

"Then why do you not ride away to your home?" asked Janet. 302

"Ah, that I can not do unless some fair maiden is brave enough to help me. In three ways she must prove her courage. First she must will to meet me here in the enchanted moorland. That you have done," declared the knight. Then he stopped, and looked pleadingly at Janet. All her fear vanished, and she asked, "In what other ways must the maiden show her courage?"

84

"She must banish all fear of him. That, too, you have done," said the knight.

"Tell me the third way, Tam Lin, for I believe I am the maid to free you."

"Only my true love can prove her courage in the third way, fair Janet."

And the maiden answered, "I am thy true love, Tam Lin."

"Then heed what I say, brave lady. To-night is Hallowe'en. At the midnight hour, the Fairy Queen and all her knights will ride abroad. If you dare win your true love, you must wait at Milescross until the Fairy Queen and her Elfin Knights pass. I shall be in her train." 303

"But how shall I know you among so many knights, Tam Lin?" then asked Lady Janet.

"I shall ride in the third group of followers. Let the first and second companies of the Fairy Queen pass, and look for me in the third. There will be only three knights in this last company; one will ride on a black horse, one on a brown, and the third on a milk-white steed," said the knight, pointing to his horse. "My right hand will be gloved, Janet," he continued, "but my left hand will hang bare at my side. By these signs you will know me."

"I shall know you without fail," nodded Janet.

"Wait, calmly, until I am near you, then spring forward and seize me. When the fairies see you holding me they will change my form into many shapes. Do not fear, but hold me fast in your arms. At last I shall take my human form. If you have courage enough to do this, you will free your true love from the power of the fairies."

"I have courage enough to do all that you say," declared Janet. Then they sealed this promise with a kiss, and parted. 304

Gloomy was the night, and eerie was the way to Milescross. But Janet threw her green mantle about her shoulders, and sped to the enchanted moorland. All the way she said to herself over and over, "On this Hallowe'en at midnight I shall free my true love, Tam Lin, from Elfland."

At Milescross she hid herself and waited. How the wind from the sea moaned across the moorland! Presently she heard a merry tinkling sound of far-off music, and in the distance she saw a twinkling light dancing forward. Janet could hear her heart beat, but there she stood, undaunted. The Fairy Queen and her train were riding forth. In the lead of her first merry company of knights and maids of honour rode the beautiful queen, whose jeweled girdle and crown flashed in the darkness. The second group passed quickly, and now came three knights in a third group. One rode on a black horse, one on a brown, and there came the milk-white steed last of all. Janet could see that one hand of the rider was gloved, and one hung bare at his side. Then up leaped the maiden. Quickly she seized the bridle of the milk-white 305 steed, pulled the rider from his horse, and threw her green mantle around him. There was a clamour among the Elfin Knights, and the Fairy Queen cried out, "Tam Lin! Tam Lin! Some mortal has hold of Tam Lin, the bonniest knight in my company!"

Then the strangest things happened. Instead of Tam Lin, Janet held in her arms a bearded lion, which struggled mightily to get away. But she remembered the knight's warning. "Hold me fast, and fear me not."

The next moment she held a fire-breathing dragon, which almost slipped from her, but she tightened her grasp, and thought of Tam Lin's words. The dragon changed to a burning bush, and the flames leaped up on all sides, but Janet stood still and felt no harm. Then in her arms she held a branching tree, filled with blossoms. And at last Tam Lin, her own true love, stood there.

When the Fairy Queen saw that none of her enchantments could frighten Janet, she cried out angrily, "The maiden has won a stately bridegroom who was my bonniest knight. Alas! Tam Lin is lost to Elfland." 306

On into the darkness rode the fairy train. Tam Lin and Lady Janet hastened back to the grey stone castle. There, in a short time, a wedding feast was prepared, and Tam Lin, who was really a Scottish Earl, and Lady Janet, the bravest maid in Scotland, were married.

—Old Ballad Retold.

307

THE COURTEOUS PRINCE

Once upon a time a bonnie Prince fell in love with a lassie who was nobly born, but was not his equal in rank. The king was sorely vexed, because his son looked with favour on this maiden, and his majesty determined to part the lovers. He sent the high chancellor of the court to an old witch for advice. After thinking the matter over for nine days, the old woman muttered the following answer:

"The lassie will I charm away
'Till courtesy doth win the day."

"I'm not quite sure what the old hag means," said the king. "But if she'll get this maiden out of the Prince's sight, I can arrange for his marriage with some one of his own rank."

In a few days the lassie disappeared, and the Prince could find no trace of her. He was very sad, indeed, and declared if he could not 308 marry his own true love he would remain single all his life.

It happened one fine day near the end of October that the young Prince and a party of nobles went hunting. The hounds were soon on the track of a fine deer, which was so wily and fleet of foot that the nobles, one by one, lost track of the quarry, and dropped out of the chase. The young Prince, who was a famous rider, continued the hunt alone. Miles and miles over the low hills he galloped until at last in the depths of a wooded glen the exhausted deer was brought to bay by the hounds, and dispatched by the Prince.

Not until after the prize was won did the royal hunter realize how dusky it was in the glen, and how threatening the evening sky looked. He felt sure he was too far from the palace to retrace his journey; besides, he had lost all trace of direction. He threw the quarry over his steed's back, whistled to his hounds, and rode slowly down the wooded valley, wondering where he could lodge for the night. 309

"Little sign of hospitality in this lonely place," he mused. "Perhaps I'd better make the best of it, and find shelter in one of the rocky hollows."

On he rode in the gathering darkness. A turn in the valley brought him to a stretch of moorland, and a little distance away he saw the dark outline of an old, deserted hunting hall.

"A cheerless looking inn," thought the Prince. "No doubt one will have to play host as well as guest here. However, I have my trusty hounds and noble steed for company, and the quarry will furnish a good meal for all of us."

He leaped from his horse and walked up to the old ruin. With very little effort he broke open the door. The creaking of its rusty hinges made strange echoings throughout the hall. The Prince led his horse into one of the small rooms, then with his hounds he went into the large dining hall, where he lit a fire on the great hearth, and proceeded to cook some venison for supper.

86

While he was waiting for the meat on the spit to roast, he listened 310 to the rising wind, which moaned about the gloomy old ruin, and rattled the doors and windows unceasingly. The good steed, in the adjoining room, pawed the floor restlessly, and every few moments the hounds stretched their heads straight up into the air, and whined in a most uncanny way.

As he mused before the fire, the Prince thought, "This is All Hallowe'en, the night when ghosts and witches hold their revels. Nevertheless, I'd rather be in this deserted hall than on the storm-swept moorland."

He took the roasted meat from the fire, and prepared to eat his supper. Suddenly a fierce blast of wind burst open a large door at the far end of the hall, and into the room stalked a tall, ghostly woman. Her lank figure was clothed in grey garments, which trailed for yards on the floor. Her long, grey hair hung loose down her back. By the light of the flickering fire the Prince could see her hollow eyes and wan features. He was a brave man, but this ghostly creature filled him with dread and horror. The hounds dropped their bones of venison, and crept close to their master, who was unable to utter a word. 311

Slowly down the hall the grey ghost glided to the Prince, and pointing a long, bony finger at him, she asked in a hollow voice, "Art thou a courteous knight?"

In a trembling voice the Prince answered, "I will serve thee. What dost thou wish?"

"Go ye to the moorland, and pluck enough heather to make a bed in the turret-room for me," said the phantom-like figure.

It was a strange request to make, but the Prince was relieved to have any excuse to get out of her sight. He sprang quickly to his feet, and hurried out to face the stormy night in search of heather. He plucked as much as he could carry in his plaid, and returned to the hall where the ghostly visitor was waiting for him. She led the way down the room, and up a half-ruined staircase to the turret-room. Here the Prince spread a heather bed for her, and covered it with his plaid. When it was finished she pointed to the door, and dismissed him.

"May you sleep well," said the Prince courteously. Then, cold and 312 weary, he descended to the hall, and lay down to sleep in front of the dying embers of the fire.

When he awakened the bright sun was shining in the windows.

The Prince lost no time in making ready to depart, for he remembered quite well the ghostly visitor of the past night.

"No doubt she departed before the crowing of the cock," he said. "I wonder if she left my bonnie plaid in the turret room. The autumn air is keen and biting. I'll go and see."

He ran quickly up the ruined staircase. To his surprise when he reached the top, the door of the chamber opened, and there before him stood his lost sweetheart.

"How camest thou here?" gasped the Prince. "And where is the grey ghost."

"Last night I was the grey ghost," she said.

"And thou wilt change thy form again to-night?" he asked in horror.

"Never again," said the maiden. "In order to part us a wicked witch threw a spell over me—a spell which changed me into the awful 313 shape thou sawest last night. But thou hast broken her wicked charm."

"Tell me how," said the Prince, whose face was beaming with happiness.

"The witch's charm could not be broken until some knight should serve me, even though my form was horrible. By thy courtesy thou hast broken the spell," said the maiden.

So the Prince and his true love rode away, and were happily married, and when the king heard of his son's adventure in the hunting hall he said, "Now I know what that old witch meant by her prophecy."

Scotch legend.

314

JACK-O'-LANTERN SONG

Upon one wild and windy night——
Woo-oo, woo-oo, woo-oo, woo-oo——
We Jacks our lanterns all did light;
The wind—it surely knew—FOR——
Whistle and whistle—and whist! Now list!
Woo-oo, woo-oo, woo-oo, woo-oo——
Whirling and twirling, with turn and twist,
The wind—it softly blew.
It was the creepiest, scariest night——
Woo-oo, woo-oo, woo-oo, woo-oo,
We held our breath, then lost it quite;
The wind—it surely knew—FOR——
Whistle and whistle—and whist! Now list!
Woo-oo, woo-oo, woo-oo, woo-oo——
Whirling and twirling, with turn and twist,
The wind—it loudly blew.
It rose in all its main and might
Woo-oo, woo-oo, woo-oo, woo-oo——
It blew out every single light;
The Wind—it surely knew—FOR——

315

Whistle and whistle—and whist! Now list!
Woo-oo, woo-oo, woo-oo, woo-oo——
Whirling and twirling, with turn and twist,
That wind—it laughed—Ho-oh!

316

317

318

A HARVEST OF THANKSGIVING STORIES

These are things I prize
And hold of dearest worth:
Light of the sapphire skies,
Peace of the silent hills,
Shelter of forests, comfort of the grass,
Music of birds, murmur of little rills,
Shadow of clouds that swiftly pass,
And, after showers,
The smell of flowers
And of the good brown earth,——
And best of all, along the way, friendship and mirth.
So let me keep

These treasures of the humble heart
In true possession, owning them by love.
Henry Van Dyke.
(Selection from God of the Open Air.)
Used by permission and special arrangement
with Chas. Scribner and Sons.
319

THE QUEER LITTLE BAKER MAN

Phila Butler Bowman

All the children were glad when the Little Baker came to town and hung the sign above his queer little brown shop,

"Thanksgiving Loaves to Sell."

Each child ran to tell the news to another child until soon the streets echoed with the sound of many running feet, and the clear November air was full of the sound of happy laughter, as a crowd of little children thronged as near as they dared to the Little Baker's shop, while the boldest crept so close that they could feel the heat from the big brick oven, and see the gleaming rows of baker's pans.

The Little Baker never said a word. He washed his hands at the 320 windmill water spout and dried them, waving them in the crisp air. Then he unfolded a long, spotless table, and setting it up before his shop door, he began to mold the loaves, while the wondering children grew nearer and nearer to watch him.

He molded big, long loaves, and tiny, round loaves; wee loaves filled with currants, square loaves with queer markings on them, fat loaves and flat loaves, and loaves in shapes such as the children had never seen before, and always as he molded he sang a soft tune to these words:

"Buy my loaves of brown and white,
Molded for the child's delight.
Who forgets another's need,
Eats unthankful and in greed;
But the child who breaks his bread
With another, Love has fed."

By and by the children began to whisper to each other.

"I shall buy that very biggest loaf," said the Biggest Boy. "Mother lets me buy what I wish. I shall eat it alone, which is fair if I pay for it." 321

"Oh," said the Tiniest Little Girl, "that would be greedy. You could never eat so big a loaf alone."

"If I pay for it, it is mine," said the Biggest Boy, boastfully, "and one need not share what is his own unless he wishes."

"Oh," said the Tiniest Little Girl, but she said it more softly this time, and she drew away from the Biggest Boy, and looked at him with eyes that had grown big and round.

"I have a penny," she said to the Little Lame Boy, "and you and I can have one of those wee loaves together. They have currants in them, so we shall not mind if the loaf is small."

"No, indeed," said the Little Lame Boy, whose face had grown wistful when the Biggest Boy had talked of the great loaf. "No, indeed, but you shall take the bigger piece."

Then the little Baker Man raked out the bright coals from the great oven into an iron basket, and he put in the loaves, every one, while the children crowded closer with eager faces. 322

When the last loaf was in, he shut the oven door with a clang so loud and merry that the children broke into a shout of laughter.

Then the Queer Little Baker Man came and stood in his tent door, and he was smiling, and he sang again a merry little tune to these words:

"Clang, clang, my oven floor,
My loaves will bake as oft before,
And you may play where shines the sun
Until each loaf is brown and done."

Then away ran the children, laughing, and looking at the door of the shop where the Queer Little Baker stood, and where the raked-out coals, bursting at times, cast long, red lights against the brown wall, and as they ran they sang together the Queer Little Baker's merry song:

"Clang, clang, my oven floor,
The loaves will bake as oft before."

Then some played at hide-and-seek among the sheaves of ungarnered corn, and some ran gleefully through the heaped-up leaves of 323 russet and gold for joy to hear them rustling. But some, eager, returned home for pennies to buy a loaf when the Queer Little Baker should call.

"The loaves are ready, white and brown,
For every little child in town,
Come buy Thanksgiving loaves and eat,
But only Love can make them sweet."

Soon all the air was filled with the sound of the swift running feet, as the children flew like a cloud of leaves blown by the wind in answer to the Queer Little Baker's call. When they came to his shop they paused, laughing and whispering, as the Little Baker laid out the loaves on the spotless table.

"This is mine," said the Biggest Boy, and laying down a silver coin he snatched the great loaf, and ran away to break it by himself.

Then came the Impatient Boy, crying: "Give me my loaf. This is mine, and give it to me at once. Do you not see my coin is silver? Do not keep me waiting."

The Little Baker never said a word. He did not smile, he did not 324 frown, he did not hurry. He gave the Impatient Boy his loaf and watched him, as he, too, hurried away to eat his loaf alone.

Then came others, crowding, pushing with their money, the strongest and rudest gaining first place, and snatching each a loaf they ran off to eat without a word of thanks, while some very little children looked on wistfully, not able even to gain a place. All this time the Queer Little Baker kept steadily on laying out the beautiful loaves on the spotless table.

A Gentle Lad came, when the crowd grew less, and giving all the pennies he had he bought loaves for all the little ones; so that by and by no one was without a loaf. The Tiniest Little Girl went away hand in hand with the Little Lame Boy to share his wee loaf, and both were smiling, and whoever broke one of those smallest loaves found it larger than it had seemed at first.

But now the biggest Boy was beginning to frown.

"This loaf is sour," he said angrily.

"But is it not your own loaf," said the Baker, "and did you not 325 choose it yourself, and choose to eat it alone? Do not complain of the loaf since it is your own choosing."

Then those who had snatched the loaves ungratefully and hurried away, without waiting for a word of thanks, came back.

"We came for good bread," they cried, "but those loaves are sodden and heavy."

"See the lad there with all those children. His bread is light. Give us, too, light bread and sweet."

But the Baker smiled a strange smile. "You chose in haste," he said, "as those choose who have no thought in sharing. I can not change your loaves. I can not choose for you. Had you, buying, forgotten that mine are Thanksgiving loaves? I shall come again; then you can buy more wisely."

Then these children went away thoughtfully.

But the very little children and the Gentle Lad sat eating their bread with joyous laughter, and each tiny loaf was broken into many pieces as they shared with each other, and to them the bread was as fine as cake and as sweet as honey. 326

Then the Queer Little Baker brought cold water and put out the fire. He folded his spotless table, and took down the boards of his little brown shop, packed all into his wagon, and drove away singing a quaint tune. Soft winds rustled the corn, and swept the boughs together with a musical chuckling. And where the brown leaves were piled thickest, making a little mound, sat the Tiniest Little Girl and the Little Lame Boy, eating their sweet currant loaf happily together.

327

A TURKEY FOR THE STUFFING

Katherine Grace Hulbert

It always made Ben feel solemn to watch the river in a storm. To-day it was grey, and rough and noisy, and the few boats, which went down toward Lake Huron, pitched about so that their decks slanted first one way, then another, and their sides were coated with ice.

"Gran'ma, what day's to-day?" he asked at last, turning from the stormy river to glance about their warm, comfortable little room.

"Wednesday, Benny," answered the small old woman who crouched over the stove.

"Then to-morrow will be Thanksgiving day, and the Rosses are going to have a turkey," said Ben, excitedly. "What are we going to have, Gran'ma?"

Mrs. Moxon looked over her glasses at her grandson's small, thin figure in its patched and faded clothes, and at his bright, eager face.

"Sonny, dear, what do you think Gran'ma has for Thanksgiving?" she asked gently.
328

The expectant look faded from Ben's face, and he winked hard to keep the tears from running over. He did not need to be told how bare of dainties their cupboard was, for everything there he had brought with his own hands. Bacon and smoked fish enough for all winter were stored away; flour, potatoes, and a few other vegetables were there.

"Tell me about a real Thanksgiving dinner," the small boy begged after the first disappointment had been bravely put away. Mrs. Moxon took off her spectacles, and leaned back cautiously in her broken-rockered chair.

"I remember one Thanksgiving when your pa was alive, we had a dinner fit for a king. There was a ten-pound turkey, with bread stuffing. I put the sage and onions into the stuffing with my own hands."

"We could have some stuffing," interrupted Ben, eagerly.

"So we could, sonny, so we could. It takes you to think of things," and Mrs. Moxon affectionately patted the little brown hand on her 329 knee. "It never would 'a' come to me that we might have turkey stuffing even if we didn't have any turkey."

Ben beamed with delight at this praise. "And was there anything else besides the turkey and the stuffing, Gran'ma?"

"Land, yes, child. There was turnips, and mashed potatoes and mince pie, and your pa got two pounds of grapes, though grapes was expensive at that time o' year. Yes, nobody could ask for a better dinner than that was."

"We could have one just like it, all but the turkey and the mince pie and the grapes," said Ben hopefully.

"So we can, and will, too, child," answered the old woman. "Trust you for making the best of things," and the two smiled at each other happily.

Next morning Ben watched his grandmother add an egg, some sage and chopped onion to a bowlful of dry bread, pour boiling water over it, and put the mixture in the oven.

"Your father said I made the best turkey stuffing he ever ate," she said with satisfaction. "We'll see how it comes out, Benny." 330

"I can't hardly wait till dinner-time," Ben said, with an excited skip. "I b'lieve I'll go down to the beach, and pick up driftwood for a while. You call me when the things are most cooked, Gran'ma."

The storm of the day before had left many a bit of board or end of a log on the beach that would be just the thing for Mrs. Moxon's stove. Ben worked so hard that he did not notice a big barge that was coming slowly down the river, towing two other boats behind it, until he heard a voice ask:

"Hullo, kid! What makes you work so hard on Thanksgiving day?"

Then he straightened up, to see the boat's captain standing near its pilot house, and shouting through a great trumpet.

"I'm waiting for dinner to cook," Ben answered in his piping voice.

"Can't hear you!" roared the captain. "Run home and get your horn, and talk to me."

Ben ran up the little hill to Mrs. Ross's, and borrowed her trumpet, or megaphone. One's voice sounds much louder when these are used, and they are to be found at every house on the shores of the St. Mary's, 331 boats, and those on the land, often want to say, "How do you do?" to each other. It was all Ben could do to hold the great tin trumpet on straight, for it was nearly as long as he was.

"I'm waiting for dinner to cook," the boy shouted again, and this time the captain heard him.

"Going to have turkey, I suppose?" the captain asked.

"No, but we're going to have turkey stuffing," answered Ben with pride.

"Turkey stuffing, but no turkey! If that isn't the best I ever heard!" The captain had dropped his trumpet, and doubled up with sudden laughter. Luckily Ben did not hear. "What else are you going to have?" he called when he had repeated the joke about him. "Mince pie without any mince meat?"

"No, sir!" Ben's voice was shrill, but clear. "My father had mince pie for Thanksgiving dinner once, though."

"Did, did he?" The captain dropped his trumpet again. "That boy's all right," he said to the first mate. "He's too plucky to be laughed at. 332 I'm going to send him some turkey for his stuffing, Morgan. Tell the cook to get ready half a turkey and a mince pie, and say, Morgan, have him send up one of those small baskets of grapes. We'll tie them to a piece of plank, and they'll float ashore all right. Tell the cook to hurry, or we'll be too far downstream for the boy to get the things." Then he raised his trumpet again.

"Say, kid, can you row that boat that's tied to your dock?"

"Yes, sir."

"Well, you hurry out into the river, and I'll put off a float with some things for your Thanksgiving dinner. You're going to have some turkey for that stuffing."

You may be sure Ben lost no time in pushing the rowboat off into the stream, where the end of a plank and its delicious load were soon bobbing up and down on the water. How he did smack his lips when he lifted them into the boat, and how pleased he was for grandma!

"First the stuffing, and then the turkey! My, ain't I lucky?" He did not know that the captain had said he was plucky, and that luck is very apt to follow pluck.

333

PUMPKIN PIE

Through sun and shower the pumpkin grew,
When the days were long and the skies were blue.
And it felt quite vain when its giant size
Was such that it carried away the prize
At the County Fair, when the people came,
And it wore a ticket and bore a name.
Alas for the pumpkin's pride! One day
A boy and his mother took it away.
It was pared and sliced and pounded and stewed,
And the way it was treated was hard and rude.
It was sprinkled with sugar and seasoned with spice,
The boy and his mother pronounced it nice.
It was served in a paste, it was baked and browned,
And at last on a pantry shelf was found.

334

And on Thursday John, Mary, and Mabel
Will see it on aunty's laden table.
For the pumpkin grew 'neath a summer sky
Just to turn at Thanksgiving into pie!
Mary Mapes Dodge.

335

MRS. NOVEMBER'S DINNER PARTY[1

By Agnes Carr

The Widow November was very busy indeed this year. What with elections and harvest homes, her hands were full to overflowing; for she takes great interest in politics, besides being a social body, without whom no apple bee or corn husking is complete.

Still, worn out as she was, when her thirty sons and daughters clustered round, and begged that they might have their usual family dinner on Thanksgiving day, she could not find it in her hospitable heart to refuse, and immediately invitations were sent to her eleven brothers and sisters, old Father Time, and Mother Year, to come with all their families and celebrate the great American holiday. 336

Then what a busy time ensued! What a slaughter of unhappy barnyard families—turkeys, ducks, and chickens! What a chopping of apples and boiling of doughnuts! What a picking of raisins and rolling of pie crust, until every nook and corner of the immense storeroom was stocked with "savoury mince and toothsome pumpkin pies," while so great was the confusion that even the stolid redhued servant, Indian Summer, lost his head, and smoked so continually he always appeared surrounded by a blue mist, as he piled logs upon the great bonfires in the yard, until they lighted up the whole country for miles around.

But at length all was ready; the happy days had come, and all the little Novembers, in their best "bib and tucker," were seated in a row, awaiting the arrival of their uncles, aunts, and cousins, while their mother, in russet-brown silk trimmed with misty lace, looked them over, straightening Guy Fawkes' collar, tying Thanksgiving's neck ribbon, and settling a dispute between two little presidential candidates as to which should sit at the head of the table. 337

Soon a merry clashing of bells, blowing of horns, and mingling of voices were heard outside, sleighs and carriages dashed up to the door, and in came, "just in season," Grandpa Time, with Grandma Year leaning on his arm, followed by all their children and grandchildren, and were warmly welcomed by the hostess and her family.

"Oh, how glad I am we could all come to-day!" said Mr. January, in his crisp, clear tones, throwing off his great fur coat, and rushing to the blazing fire. "There is nothing like the happy returns of these days."

"Nothing, indeed," simpered Mrs. February, the poetess. "If I had had time I should have composed some verses for the occasion; but my son Valentine has brought a sugar heart, with a sweet sentiment on it, to his cousin Thanksgiving. I, too, have taken the liberty of bringing a sort of adopted child of mine, young Leap Year, who makes us a visit every four years."

"He is very welcome, I am sure," said Mrs. November, patting Leap Year kindly on the head. "And, Sister March, how have you been since we last met?" 338

"Oh! we have had the North, South, East, and West Winds all at our house, and they have kept things breezy, I assure you. But I really feared we should not get here to-day; for when we came to dress I found nearly everything we had was lent; so that must account for our shabby appearance."

"He! he! he!" tittered little April Fool. "What a sell!" And he shook until the bells on his cap rang; at which his father ceased for a moment showering kisses on his nieces and nephews, and boxed his ears for his rudeness.

"Oh, Aunt May! do tell us a story," clamoured the younger children, and dragging her into a corner she was soon deep in such a moving tale that they were all melted to tears, especially the little Aprils, who cry very easily.

Meanwhile, Mrs. June, assisted by her youngest daughter, a "sweet girl graduate," just from school, was engaged in decking the apartment with roses and lilies and other fragrant flowers that she had brought from her extensive gardens and conservatories, until the 339 room was a perfect bower of sweetness and beauty; while Mr. July draped the walls with flags and banners, lighted the candles, and showed off the tricks of his pet eagle, Yankee Doodle, to the great delight of the little ones.

Madam August, who suffers a great deal with the heat, found a seat on a comfortable sofa, as far from the fire as possible, and waved a huge feather fan back and forth, while her thirty-one boys and girls, led by the two oldest, Holiday and Vacation, ran riot through the long rooms, picking at their Aunt June's flowers, and playing all sorts of pranks, regardless of tumbled hair and torn clothes, while they shouted, "Hurrah for fun!" and behaved like a pack of wild colts let loose in a green pasture, until their Uncle September called them, together with his own children, into the library, and persuaded them to read some of the books with which the shelves were filled, or play quietly with the game of Authors and the Dissected Maps.

"For," said Mr. September to Mrs. October, "I think Sister August lets her children romp too much. I always like improving games for mine, although I have great trouble in making Equinox toe the line as he should." 340

"That is because you are a schoolmaster," laughed Mrs. October, shaking her head, adorned with a wreath of gaily tinted leaves; "but where is my baby?"

At that moment a cry was heard without, and Indian Summer came running in to say that little All Hallows had fallen into a tub of water while trying to catch an apple that was floating on top, and Mrs. October, rushing off to the kitchen, returned with her youngest in a very wet and dripping condition, and screaming at the top of his lusty little lungs. He could only be consoled by a handful of chestnuts, which his nurse, Miss Frost, cracked open for him.

The little Novembers, meanwhile, were having a charming time with their favourite cousins, the Decembers, who were always so gay and jolly, and had such a delightful papa. He came with his pockets stuffed full of toys and sugarplums, which he drew out from time to time, and gave to his best-loved child, Merry Christmas, to 341 distribute amongst the children, who gathered eagerly around their little cousin, saying:

"Christmas comes but once a year,
But when she comes she brings good cheer."

At which Merry laughed gaily, and tossed her golden curls, in which were twined sprays of holly and clusters of brilliant scarlet berries.

At last the great folding-doors were thrown open. Indian summer announced that dinner was served, and a long procession of old and young was quickly formed, and led by Mrs. November and her daughter Thanksgiving, whose birthday it was. They filed into the spacious dining-room, where stood the long table, groaning beneath its weight of good things, while four servants ran continually in and out bringing more substantials and delicacies to grace the board and please the appetite. Winter staggered beneath great trenchers of meat and poultry, pies, and puddings; Spring brought the earliest and freshest vegetables; Summer, the richest creams and ices; while Autumn served the guests with fruit, and poured the sparkling wine. 342

All were gay and jolly, and many a joke was cracked as the contents of each plate and dish melted away like snow before the sun, and the great fires roared in the wide chimneys as though singing a glad Thanksgiving song.

New Year drank everybody's health, and wished them "many returns of the day," while Twelfth Night ate so much cake he made himself quite ill, and had to be put to bed.

Valentine sent mottoes to all the little girls, and praised their bright eyes and glossy curls. "For," said his mother, "he is a sad flatterer, and not nearly so truthful, I am sorry to say, as his brother, George Washington, who never told a lie."

At which Grandfather Time gave George a quarter, and said he should always remember what a good boy he was.

After dinner the fun increased, all trying to do something for the general amusement. Mrs. March persuaded her son, St. Patrick, to dance an Irish Jig, which he did to the tune of the "Wearing of the Green," 343 which his brothers, Windy and Gusty, blew and whistled on their fingers.

Easter sang a beautiful song, the little Mays, "tripped the light fantastic toe" in a pretty fancy dance, while the Junes sat by so smiling and sweet it was a pleasure to look at them.

95

Independence, the fourth child of Mr. July, who is a bold little fellow, and a fine speaker, gave them an oration he had learned at school; and the Augusts suggested games of tag and blindman's buff, which they all enjoyed heartily.

Mr. September tried to read an instructive story aloud, but was interrupted by Equinox, April Fool, and little All Hallows, who pinned streamers to his coat tails, covered him with flour, and would not let him get through a line; at which Mrs. October hugged her tricksy baby, and laughed until she cried, and Mr. September retired in disgust.

"That is almost too bad," said Mrs. November, as she shook the popper vigorously in which the corn was popping and snapping merrily; "but, 344 Thanksgiving, you must not forget to thank your cousins for all they have done to honour your birthday."

At which the demure little maiden went round to each one, and returned her thanks in such a charming way it was quite captivating.

Grandmother Year at last began to nod over her teacup in the chimney corner.

"It is growing late," said Grandpa Time.

"But we must have a Virginia Reel before we go," said Mr. December.

"Oh, yes, yes!" cried all the children.

Merry Christmas played a lively air on the piano, and old and young took their positions on the polished floor with grandpa and grandma at the head.

Midsummer danced with Happy New Year, June's Commencement with August's Holiday, Leap Year with May Day, and all "went merry as a marriage bell."

The fun was at its height when suddenly the clock in the corner struck twelve. Grandma Year motioned all to stop, and Grandfather Time, bowing his head, said softly, "Hark! my children, Thanksgiving Day is ended."

[1 From Harper's Young People, November, 1883.

345
THE DEBUT OF "DAN'L WEBSTER"

Isabel Gordon Curtis
Used by permission of St. Nicholas.

"I guess you can get the ell roof shingled now, 'most any old time," cried Homer Tidd. He bounced in at the kitchen door. A blast of icy wind followed him.

"Gracious! shet the door, Homer, an' then tell me your news." His mother shivered and pulled a little brown shawl tighter about her shoulders. The boy planted himself behind the stove and laid his mittened hands comfortably around the pipe. "Oh, I've made a great deal, Mother." Homer's freckled face glowed with satisfaction.

"What?" asked Mrs. Tidd.

"Did you see the man that jest druv out o' the yard?"

"No, I didn't, Homer."

346 "Well, 'twas Mr. Richards—the Mr. Richards o' Finch & Richards, the big market folks over in the city."

"Has he bought your Thanksgivin' turkeys?"

"He hain't bought 'em for Thanksgivin'."

"Well, what are you so set up about, boy?"

"He's rented the hull flock. He's to pay me three dollars a day for them, then he's goin' to buy them all for Christmas."

"Land sakes! Three dollars a day." Mrs. Tidd dropped one side of a pan of apples she was carrying, and some of them went rolling about the kitchen floor.

Homer nodded.

"For how long?" she asked eagerly.

"For a week." Homer's freckles disappeared in the crimson glow of enthusiasm that overspread his face.

"Eighteen dollars for nothin' but exhibitin' a bunch o' turkeys! Seems to me some folks must have money to throw away." Mrs. Tidd stared perplexedly over the top of her glasses.

"I'll tell you all about it, Mother." Homer took a chair and planted 347 his feet on the edge of the oven. "Mr. Richards is goin' to have a great Thanksgivin' food show, an' he wants a flock o' live turkeys. He's been drivin' round the country lookin' for some. The postmaster sent him here. He told him about Dan'l Webster's tricks."

"They don't make Dan'l any better eatin'," objected his mother.

"Maybe not. But don't you see? Well!"

Homer's laugh was an embarrassed one. "I'm goin' to put Dan'l an' Gettysburg through their tricks right in the store window."

"You ben't?" and the mother looked in rapt admiration at her clever son.

"I be!" answered Homer, triumphantly.

"I don't know, boy, jest what I think o' it," said his mother, slowly. "'Tain't exactly a—a gentlemanly sort o' thing to do; be it?"

"I reckon I ben't a gentleman, Mother," replied Homer, with his jolly laugh.

"Tell me all about it."

"Well, I was feedin' the turkeys when Mr. Richards druv in. He said he heered I had some trick turkeys, an' he'd like to see 'em. Lucky 348 enough, I hadn't fed 'em; they was awful hungry, an' I tell you they never did their tricks better."

"What did Mr. Richards say?"

"He thought it was the most amazin' thing he'd ever seen in his life. He said he wouldn't have believed turkeys had enough gumption in them to learn a trick o' any kind."

"Did you tell him how you'd fussed with them ever since they was little chicks?"

"I did. He wuz real interested, an' he offered me three dollars to give a show three times a day. He's got a window half as big as this kitchen. He'll have it wired in, an' the turkeys'll stay there at his expense. Along before Christmas he'll give me twenty-two cents a pound for 'em."

"Well, I vow, Homer, it's pretty good pay."

"Mr. Richards give me a commutation on the railroad. He's to send after the turkeys an' bring 'em back, so I won't have any expense."

Homer rose and sauntered about the kitchen, picking up the apples that had rolled in all directions over the floor. 349

A week before Thanksgiving, the corner in front of Finch & Richard's great market looked as it was wont to look on circus day: only the eyes of the crowds were not turned expectantly up Main Street; they were riveted on a window in the big store. Passers-by tramped out into the snowy street when they reached the mob at the corner. The front of the store was decorated with a fringe of plump turkeys. One window had held a glowing mountain of fruit and vegetables arranged by someone with a keen eye to colour— monstrous pumpkins, splendid purple cabbages, rosy apples and russet pears, green and purple grapes, snowy stalks of celery, and corn ears yellow as sunshine. Crimson beets neighboured with snowy parsnips, scarlet carrots, and silk-wrapped onions. Egg-plants, gleaming like deep-hued amethysts, circled about magnificent cauliflowers, while red and yellow bananas made gay mosaic walks through the fruit mountain. Wherever a crack or a cranny had been left was a mound of ruby cranberries, fine raisin bunches, or brown nuts. 350

It was a remarkable display of American products; yet, after the first "Ah" of admiration, people passed on to the farther window, where six plump turkeys, supremely innocent of a feast-day fête, flapped their wings or gobbled impertinently when a small boy laid his nose flat against the window. Three times a day the crowd grew twenty deep. It laughed and shouted and elbowed one another good-naturedly, for the Thanksgiving spirit was abroad. Men tossed children up on their stalwart shoulders, then small hands clapped ecstatically, and small legs kicked with wild enthusiasm.

The hero of the hour was a freckled, redhaired boy, who came leaping through a wire door with an old broom over his shoulders. Every turkey waited for him eagerly, hungrily! They knew that each old, familiar trick—learned away back in chickhood— would earn a good feed. When the freckled boy began to whistle, or when his voice rang out in a shrill order, it was the signal for Dan'l Webster, for Gettysburg, for Amanda Ann, Mehitable, Nancy, or Farragut to step to 351 the center of the stage and do some irresistibly funny turn with a turkey's bland solemnity. None of the birds had attacks of stage fright—their acting was as self-possessed as if they were in the old farm yard with no audience present but Mrs. Tidd to lean smiling over the fence with a word of praise, and the coveted handful of golden corn.

With every performance the crowd grew more dense, the applause more uproarious, and the Thanksgiving trade at Finch & Richard's bigger than it had been in years. Each night Homer took the last train home, tired but happy, for three crisp greenbacks were added to the roll in his small, shabby wallet.

Two days before Thanksgiving, Homer, in his blue overalls and faded sweater, was busy at work. The gray of the dawn was just creeping into the east, while the boy went hurrying through his chores. There was still a man's work to be done before he took the ten o'clock train to town; besides, he had promised to help his mother about the house. His grandfather, an uncle, an aunt, and three small cousins were coming to eat their Thanksgiving feast at the old farmhouse. 352 Homer whistled gaily, while he bedded the creatures with fresh straw. The whistle trailed into an indistinct trill; the boy felt a pang of loneliness as he glanced into the turkey-pen. There was nobody there but old Mother Salvia. Homer tossed her a handful of corn. "Poor old lady, I s'pose you're lonesome, ain't you, now? Never mind; when spring comes you'll be scratchin' around with a hull raft of nice little chickies at your heels. We'll teach them a fine trick or two, won't we, old Salvia?"

Salvia clucked over the corn appreciatively.

"Homer, Homer, come here quick."

Down the frozen path through the yard came Mrs. Tidd, with the little brown shawl wrapped tightly about her head. She fluttered a yellow envelope in her hand.

"Homer boy, it's a telegraph come. I can't read it; I've mislaid my glasses."

Homer was by her side in a minute, tearing open the flimsy envelope.

"It's from Finch & Richards, Mother," he cried excitedly. "They say, 'Take the first train to town without fail.'" 353

"What do you s'pose they want you for?" asked Mrs. Tidd, with a very anxious face.

"P'r'aps the store's burned down," gasped Homer. He brushed one rough hand across his eyes. "Poor Dan'l Webster an' Gettysburg! I didn't know anybody could set so much store by turkeys."

"Maybe 't ain't nothin' bad, Homer," Mrs. Tidd laid her hand upon his shoulder. "Maybe they want you to give an extra early show or somethin'." She suggested it cheerfully.

"Maybe," echoed Homer. "But, Mother, I've got to hurry to catch that 7:30 train."

"Let me go with you, Homer."

"You don't need to," cried the boy. "It probably ain't nothin' serious."

"I'm goin'," cried Mrs. Tidd decisively; "you don't s'pose I could stay here doin' nothin' but waitin' an' wond'rin'?"

Mrs. Tidd and Homer caught a car at the city depot. Five minutes later they stood in front of Finch & Richards' big market.

"Mother," whispered the boy, as he stepped off the car, "Mother, my 354 turkeys! They're not there! Something's happened. See the crowd."

They pushed their way through a mob that was peering in at the windows, and through the windows of locked doors. The row of plump turkeys was not hung this morning under the big sign; the magnificent window display of fruit and vegetables had been ruthlessly demolished.

"What do you s'pose can have happened?" whispered Mrs. Tidd, while they waited for a clerk to come hurrying down the store and unlock the door.

Homer shook his head.

Mr. Richards himself came to greet them.

"Well, young man," he cried, "I've had enough of your pesky bird show. There's a hundred dollars' worth of provisions gone, to say nothing of the trade we are turning away. Two days before Thanksgiving, of all times in the year!"

"Good land!" whispered Mrs. Tidd. Her eyes were wandering about the store. It was scattered from one end to the other with wasted food. 355 Sticky rivers trickled here and there across the floor. A small army of clerks was hard at work sweeping and mopping.

"Where's my turkeys?" asked Homer.

"Your turkeys, confound them!" snarled Mr. Richards. "They're safe and sound in their crate in my back store, all but that blasted old gobbler you call Dan'l Webster. He's doing his stunts on a top shelf. We found him there tearing cereal packages into shreds. For mercy's sake, go and see if you can't get him down. He has almost pecked the eyes out of every clerk who has tried to lay a finger on him. I'd like to wring his ugly neck."

Mr. Richard's face grew red as the comb of Dan'l Webster himself.

Homer and his mother dashed across the store. High above their heads strutted Dan'l Webster with a slow, stately tread. Occasionally he peered down at the ruin and confusion below, commenting upon it with a lordly, satisfied gobble.

"Dan'l Webster," called Homer, coaxingly, "good old Dan'l, come an' see me."

The boy slipped cautiously along to where a step-ladder stood. 356

"Dan'l," he called persuasively, "wouldn't you like to come home, Dan'l?"

Dan'l perked down with pleased recognition in his eyes. Homer crept up the ladder. He was preparing to lay a hand on one of Dan'l's black legs when the turkey hopped away with a triumphant gobble, and went racing gleefully along the wide shelf. A row of bottles filled with salad-dressing stood in Dan'l's path. He cleared them out of the way with one energetic kick. They tumbled to a lower shelf; their yellow contents crept in a sluggish stream toward the mouth of a tea-box.

"I'll have that bird shot!" thundered Mr. Richards. "That's all there is about it."

"Wait a minute, sir," pleaded Mrs. Tidd. "Homer'll get him."

Dan'l Webster would neither be coaxed nor commanded. He wandered up and down the shelf, gobbling vociferously into the faces of the excited mob.

"Henry, go and get a pistol," cried Mr. Richards, turning to one of his clerks. 357

"Homer,"—Mrs. Tidd clutched the boy's arm,—"why don't you make b'lieve you're shootin' Dan'l? Maybe he'll lie down, so you can git him."

Homer called for a broom. He tossed it, gun fashion, across his shoulder, and crept along slowly, sliding a ladder before him to the spot where the turkey stood watching with intent eyes. He put one foot upon the lowest step, then he burst out in a spirited whistle. It was "Marching through Georgia." The bird stared at him fixedly.

"Bang!" cried Homer, and he pointed the broom straight at the recreant turkey.

Dan'l Webster dropped stiff. A second later Homer had a firm grasp of the scaly legs. Dan'l returned instantly to life, but the rebellious head was tucked under his master's jacket. Dan'l Webster thought he was being strangled to death.

"There!" cried Homer, triumphantly. He closed the lid of the poultry crate, and wiped the perspiration from his forehead. "There! I guess you won't get out again."

He followed Mr. Richards to the front of the store to view the devastation. 358

"Who'd have thought turkeys could have ripped up strong wire like that?" cried the enraged market man, pointing to the shattered door.

"I guess Dan'l began the mischief," said Homer soberly; "he's awful strong."

"I'm sorry I ever laid eyes on Dan'l!" exclaimed Mr. Richards. "I'll hate to see Finch. He'll be in on the 4.20 train. He's conservative; he never had any use for the turkey show."

"When did you find out that they—what had happened?" asked Homer timidly.

"At five o'clock. Two of the men got here early. They telephoned me. I never saw such destruction in my life. Your turkeys had sampled most everything in the store, from split peas to molasses. What they didn't eat they knocked over or tore open. I guess they won't need feeding for a week. They're chuckful of oatmeal, beans, crackers, peanuts, pickles, toothpicks, prunes, soap, red herrings, cabbage—about everything their crops can hold."

"I'm awfully sorry," faltered Homer.

359 "So am I," said Mr. Richards resolutely. "Now, the best thing you can do is to take your flock and clear out. I've had enough of performing turkeys."

Homer and his mother waited at the depot for the 11 o'clock train. Beside them stood a crate filled with turkeys that wore a well-fed, satisfied expression. Somebody tapped Homer on the shoulder.

"You're the boy who does the stunts with turkeys, aren't you?" asked a well-dressed man with a silk hat, and a flower in his buttonhole.

"Yes," answered the boy, wonderingly.

"I've been hunting for you. That was a great rumpus you made at Finch & Richards'. The whole town's talking about it."

"Yes," answered Homer again, and he blushed scarlet.

"Taking your turkeys home?"

Homer nodded.

"I've come to see if we can keep them in town a few days longer."

The boy shook his head vigorously. "I don't want any more turkey shows." 360

"Not if the price is big enough to make it worth your while?"

"No!" said Homer sturdily.

"Let us go into the station and talk it over."

On Thanksgiving afternoon the Colonial Theater, the best vaudeville house in the city, held a throng that was dined well, and was happy enough to appreciate any sort of fun. The children—hundreds of them—shrieked with delight over every act. The women laughed, the men applauded with great hearty hand-claps. A little buzz of excitement went round the house when, at the end of the fourth turn, two boys, instead of setting up the regulation big red number, displayed a brand new card. It read: "Extra Number—Homer Tidd and his Performing Turkeys." A shout of delighted anticipation went up from the audience. Every paper in town had made a spectacular story of the ruin at Finch & Richards'. Nothing could have been so splendid a surprise. Everybody broke into applause, everybody except one little woman who sat in the front row of the orchestra. Her face was 361 pale, her hands clasped, and unclasped each other tremulously. "Homer, boy," she whispered to herself.

The curtain rolled up. The stage was set for a realistic farmyard scene. The floor was scattered with straw, an old pump leaned over in one corner, hay tumbled untidily from a barn-loft, a coop with a hen and chickens stood by the fence. From her stall stared a white-faced cow; her eyes blinked at the glare of the footlights. The orchestra struck up a merry tune; the cow uttered an astonished moo; then in walked a sturdy lad with fine, broad shoulders, red hair, and freckles. His boots clumped, his blue overalls were faded, his sweater had once been red. At his heels stepped six splendid turkeys, straight in line, every one with its eyes on the master. Homer never knew how he did it. Two minutes earlier he had said to the manager, desperately: "I'll cut an' run right off as soon as I set eyes on folks." Perhaps he drew courage from the anxious gaze in his mother's eyes. Hers was the only face he saw in the great audience. Perhaps it 362 was the magnificent aplomb of the turkeys that inspired him. They stepped serenely, as if walking out on a gorgeously lighted stage was an every-day event in their lives. Anyhow, Homer threw up his head, and led the turkey march round and round past the footlights, till the shout of applause dwindled into silence. The boy threw back his head and snapped his fingers. The turkeys retreated to form in line at the back of the stage.

"Gettysburg," cried Homer, pointing to a stately, plump hen. Gettysburg stepped to the center of the stage. "How many kernels of corn have I thrown you, Getty?" he asked.

The turkey turned to count them, with her head cocked reflectively on one side. Then she scratched her foot on the floor.

"One, two, three, four, five!"

"Right. Now you may eat them, Getty."

Gettysburg wore her new-won laurels with an excellent grace. She jumped through a row of hoops, slid gracefully about the stage on a pair of miniature roller-skates; she stepped from stool to chair, from chair to table, in perfect time with Homer's whistle, 363 and a low strain of melody from the orchestra. She danced a stately jig on the table, then, with a satisfied cluck, descended on the other side to the floor. Amanda Ann, Mehitable, Nancy, and Farragut achieved their triumphs in a slow dance made up of dignified hops and mazy turns. They stood in a decorous line awaiting the return of their master, for Homer had dashed suddenly from the stage. He reappeared, holding his head up proudly. Now he wore the blue uniform and jaunty cap of a soldier boy; a gun leaned on his shoulder.

The orchestra put all its vigor, patriotism, and wind into "Marching through Georgia."

Straight to Homer's side when they heard his whistle, wheeled the turkey regiment, ready to keep step, to fall in line, to march and countermarch. Only one feathered soldier fell. It was Dan'l Webster. At a bang from Homer's rifle he dropped stiff and stark. From children here and there in the audience came a cry of horror. They turned to ask in frightened whispers if the turkey was "truly shooted." As if to answer the question, Dan'l leaped to his feet. 364 Homer pulled a Stars and Stripes from his pocket, and waved it

101

enthusiastically; then the orchestra dashed into "Yankee Doodle." It awoke some patriotic spirit in the soul of Dan'l Webster. He left his master, and, puffing himself to his stateliest proportions, stalked to the footlights to utter one glorious, soul-stirring gobble. The curtain fell, but the applause went on and on and on! At last, out again across the stage came Homer, waving "Old Glory." Dan'l Webster, Gettysburg, Amanda Ann, Nancy, Mehitable and Farragut followed in a triumphal march. Homer's eyes were bent past the footlights, searching for the face of one little woman. This time the face was one radiant flush, and her hands were adding their share to the deafening applause.

"Homer, boy," she said fondly. This time she spoke aloud, but nobody heard it. An encore for the "Extra Turn" was so vociferous, it almost shook the plaster from the ceiling.

365

THE GREEN CORN DANCE

Frances Jenkins Olcott

The first Thanksgiving Dinner in America, where was it eaten? Why, of course, we think of its being eaten in old Plymouth Town, when the Pilgrim Fathers spread their board with fish, wild turkey, geese, ducks, venison, barley bread, Indian maize, and other good things, and invited the Indian King Massasoit and his braves to the feast. It was a time of rejoicing and thanksgiving for the fine harvest God had given the Pilgrims.

But that was not the first Thanksgiving Dinner eaten in America! For many, many years before the Pilgrims came to this land, Thanksgiving Dinners had been given. The Red Men, the first owners of America, held their Thanksgiving Festivals every autumn. These 366 were in celebration of the ripening of the corn, and in honour of their Manitos, as they called their gods. For, until the white men came, the Indians never heard of the all-good "Great Spirit" of Heaven. They held other feasts, too, among them a New Year one, a Maple Sugar Feast, a Strawberry Festival, a Bean Dance, and a Corn-gathering Feast.

Even to-day, some Indians keep their heathen Thanksgiving at the time of the ripening of the corn. It is called the Green Corn Dance. Many Indians are Christians, but numbers still worship the Manitos of the sun, moon, stars, wind, rain, thunder, and other things in Nature. Though some of these heathen Red Men speak reverently of the Great Spirit, they seem scarcely to understand who He is, and confuse Him with their Manitos, as may be seen in the hymn that introduces the Feather Dance.

Among some tribes of the Iroquois Family, in New York State, the Green Corn Dance is still celebrated. And this is how a visitor saw the dance at the Cattaraugus Reservation. 367

As the time for the Festival approached, certain men and women of the tribe, called the "Keepers of the Faith," began to prepare for the dance. Every morning at sunrise, the women went to the cornfield and picked a few ears, and took them to the Head Man at the Council House. When he decided that the corn was sufficiently ripe, the Feast was called.

Summons were sent to the Indians at the Tonawanda and Allegany Reservations, bidding all meet at sunrise on the tenth of September, in the Council House of the Cattaraugus Reservation.

On the morning of the feast, the men, "Keepers of the Faith," arose at sunrise, and built a fire, on which they threw an offering of tobacco and corn, and they prayed to the Great Spirit to bless the tribes. They then extinguished the fire, and later the women "Keepers of the Faith" built another in the same spot.

Then the people began to arrive, all in their best clothes. While they were waiting for the ceremonies to begin, the young men played ball, and the girls walked about, talking with each other. Meanwhile, 368 the women "Keepers of the Faith," hastened to prepare soup and succotash, which were soon boiling in large kettles suspended over huge, flaming logs.

After a little while the people began to move toward the Council House, a long, low, wooden building, with a door at the northeast end, and another at the southwest. The people entered in two lines, the women through one door, and the men through the other. All took their seats on benches arranged on three sides of the room. In the centre of the room sat the singers, and the musicians with their turtle-shell rattles.

When all was quiet, the speaker began the ceremonies by a prayer to the Great Spirit, while the men, with bowed, uncovered heads,—Indians do not kneel,—listened reverently.

After the prayer was finished, the speaker, lifting his voice, addressed the Indians.

"My friends," he said, "we are here to worship the Great Spirit. As by our old custom, we give the Great Spirit His dance, the Great Feather Dance. We must have it before noon. The Great Spirit sees to everything in the morning, afterwards he rests. He gives us 369 land and things to live on, so we must thank Him for His ground, and for the things it brought forth. He gave us the thunder to wet the land, so we must thank the thunder. We must thank Ga-ne-o-di-o[2 that we know he is in the happy land. It is the wish of the Great Spirit that we express our thanks in dances as well as prayer. The cousin clans are here from Tonawanda; we are thankful to the Great Spirit to have them here, and to greet them with the rattles and singing. We have appointed one of them to lead the dances."

When the speaker finished, there was a pause, then a shout outside the Council House told that the Feather Dancers were coming. They entered the room, a long, gracefully swaying line of fifty men, clad in Indian costume, gay with colour and nodding plumes, and with bells adorning their leggings. Slowly and majestically they entered, and stood for a moment near the entrance. Then the speaker began in a high voice, the hymn of thanksgiving to the Great Spirit, while the 370 dancers, in single file, commenced walking slowly around the room, keeping step with the beating of the musicians' rattles.

Each verse of the hymn thanked the Great Spirit for some benefit,—for water, for the animals, for the trees, for the light, for the fruits, for the stars, and among other good things, for the "Supporters," the three Manito-sisters, the guardians of the Corn, Bean, and Squash.

After each verse, the dancers quickened their steps, and danced rapidly around the room. When the hymn was finished, the speaker ordered the real dance to start. Then, still in single file, the dancers began the great Feather Dance.

Erect in body, yet gracefully swaying, they moved around and around the Council House, keeping time with the rhythmic beat of the rattles, that sounded now slow and now fast. Lifting each foot alternately from the floor, every dancer brought his heel down with such force that all the legging-bells rang in time with the music. At times the movement grew very swift, and the many lithesome twistings 371 and bendings of the dancers, their shouts to one another, and the cries of the spectators, filled all with keen excitement. During the slower movements, some of the women arose, and joined the dance, forming an inner circle.

Then the dancers sang a weird chant, in company with the singers, "Ha-ho!—Ha-ho!—Ha-ho!" they sang; then all present joined in the quick refrain, "Way-ha-ah! Way-ha-

103

ah! Way-ha-ah!" ending in a loud, guttural shout, as the dancers bowed their heads, "Ha-i! Ha-i!"

When the noon hour came, the great Feather Dance was over, and two huge kettles were brought in to the Council House, one full of soup, and the other of succotash. One of the men "Keepers of the Faith," said a prayer of thanksgiving, in which all joined, and the food was poured into vessels brought by the women. It was then carried to the homes, where the Indians enjoyed eating it by their own firesides.

The feast was over for that day, but it lasted two days more, during which the tribes gambled, danced, ate, and beat their drums. The 372 visitor who saw this Green Corn Festival, wrote afterward about the closing scene, the great Snake Dance:

"The nodding plumes, the tinkling bells, the noisy rattles, the beats of the high-strung drums, the shuffling feet and weird cries of the dancers, and the approving shouts of the spectators, all added to the spell of a strangeness that seemed to invest the quaint old Council House with the supernaturalness of a dream!

"As the sun neared its setting, the dancers stopped in a quiet order, and the speaker of the day bade farewell to the clans ... and, after invoking the blessing of the Great Spirit, declared the Green Corn Festival of 1890 ended."

[2 A prophet of the Indians.

373
THANKSGIVING

"Have you cut the wheat in the blowing fields,
The barley, the oats, and the rye,
The golden corn and the pearly rice?
For the winter days are nigh."
"We have reaped them all from shore to shore,
And the grain is safe on the threshing floor."
"Have you gathered the berries from the vine,
And the fruit from the orchard trees?
The dew and the scent from the roses and thyme,
In the hive of the honeybees?"
"The peach and the plum and the apple are ours,
And the honeycomb from the scented flowers."
"The wealth of the snowy cotton field
And the gift of the sugar cane,
The savoury herb and the nourishing root——
There has nothing been given in vain."
"We have gathered the harvest from shore to shore,
And the measure is full and brimming o'er."
374
"Then lift up the head with a song!
And lift up the hand with a gift!
To the ancient Giver of all
The spirit in gratitude lift!
For the joy and the promise of spring,
For the hay and the clover sweet,
The barley, the rye, and the oats,
The rice, and the corn, and the wheat,

The cotton, and sugar, and fruit,
The flowers and the fine honeycomb,
The country so fair and so free,
The blessings and glory of home."
Amelia E. Barr.
375

THE TWO ALMS
OR
THE THANKSGIVING DAY GIFT

Translated by special permission from Guerber's Contes et Legendes, Ière Partie. Copyright by American Book Company.

Once upon a time a poor old beggar woman stood shivering by the side of a road which led to a prosperous village. She hoped some traveler would be touched by her misery, and would give her a few pennies with which to buy food and fuel.

It had been snowing since early morning, and a sharp east wind made the evening air bitterly cold. At the sound of approaching footsteps the old woman's face brightened with expectancy, but the next moment her eager expression changed to disappointment, for the traveler passed without giving her anything.

"Poor old woman," he said to himself. "This is a bitter cold night to be begging on the roadside. It is, indeed. I am truly sorry for her." 376

And as his footsteps became fainter, the beggar woman whispered, "I must not give up. Perhaps the next traveler will help me."

In a little while she heard the sound of wheels. It happened to be the carriage of the mayor, who was on his way to a Thanksgiving banquet. When his excellency saw the miserable old woman, he ordered the carriage to stop, lowered the window, and took a piece of money from his pocket.

"Here you are, he called, holding out a coin.

The woman hurried to the window as fast as she could. Before she reached it, however, the mayor noticed that he had taken a gold piece instead of a silver one out of his pocket.

"Wait a moment," he said. "I've made a mistake."

He intended to exchange the coin for one of less value, but he caught his sleeve on the window fastening, and dropped the gold piece in the snow. The woman had come up to the carriage window, and he noticed that she was blind. 377

"I've dropped the money, my good woman," he said, "but it lies near you there in the snow. No doubt you'll find it."

"Thank you, sir, thank you," said the beggar, kneeling down to search for the coin.

On rolled the mayor to the banquet. "It was foolish to give her gold," he thought, "but I'm a rich man, and I seldom make such a mistake."

That night after the banquet when the mayor sat before a blazing fire in his comfortable chair, the picture of the beggar woman, kneeling in the snow, and fumbling around for the gold piece, came before his eyes.

"I hope she will make good use of my generous gift," he mused. "It was entirely too much to give, but no doubt I shall be rewarded for my charity."

The first traveler hurried on his way until he came to the village inn, where a great wood fire crackled merrily in the cheery dining room. He took off his warm coat, and sat down to wait for dinner to be served. But he could not forget the picture of the old beggar woman standing on the snowy roadside. 378

Suddenly he rose, put on his coat, and said to the host, "Prepare dinner for two. I shall be back presently."

He hastened back to the place where he had seen the poor old woman, who was still on her knees in the snow searching for the mayor's gold piece.

"My good woman, what are you looking for?" he asked.

"A piece of money, sir. The gentleman who gave it to me dropped it in the snow."

"Do not search any longer," said the traveler, "but come with me to the village inn. There you may warm yourself before the great fire, and we shall have a good dinner. Come, you shall be my Thanksgiving guest."

He helped her to her feet, and then, for the first time, he saw that she was blind. Carefully he took her arm, and led her along the road to the inn.

"Sit here and warm yourself," he said, placing her gently in a comfortable chair. In a few moments he led her to the table, and gave her a good dinner. 379

On that Thanksgiving Day an angel took up her pen, and struck out all account of the gold piece from the book where the mayor recorded his good deeds. Another angel wrote in the traveler's book of deeds an account of the old beggar woman's Thanksgiving dinner at the village inn.—Adapted.

380

A THANKSGIVING PSALM

Make a joyful noise unto the Lord, all ye lands.
Serve the Lord with gladness:
Come unto his presence with singing.
Know ye that the Lord he is God;
It is he that hath made us, and not we ourselves;
We are his people and the sheep of his pasture.
Enter into his gates with thanksgiving
And into his courts with praise,
Be thankful unto him, and bless his name.
For the Lord is good; his mercy is everlasting:
And his truth endureth to all generations.
—Psalm C.

381

THE CROWN OF THE YEAR

Ah, happy morning of autumn sweet,
Yet ripe and rich with summer's heat.
Near me each humble flower and weed——
The dock's rich umber, gone to seed,
The hawk-bit's gold, the bayberry's spice,
One late wild rose beyond all price;
Each is a friend and all are dear,
Pathetic signs of the waning year.
The painted rose-leaves, how they glow!
Like crimson wine the woodbines show;
The wholesome yarrow's clusters fine,
Like frosted silver dimly shine;

And who thy quaintest charm shall tell,
Thou little scarlet pimpernel?
In the mellow, golden autumn days,
When the world is zoned in their purple haze,
A spirit of beauty walks abroad,
That fills the heart with peace of God;
The spring and summer may bless and cheer,
But autumn brings us the crown o' the year.
Celia Thaxter.